THE PROFESSOR'S DRAGON

A Here Be Dragons Novel

LOUISA MASTERS

The Professor's Dragon

Copyright © 2021 by Louisa Masters

Cover: Booksmith Design

Editor: Hot Tree Editing

All rights reserved.

No part of this book may be reproduced in any form or by any means without the prior written consent of the author, excepting brief quotes used in reviews.

This is a work of fiction. Names, characters, places, events and incidents either are the product of the author's imagination or are used fictitiously, and any resemblance to persons, living or dead, business establishments, events or locales is entirely coincidental.

To the extent that the image or images on the cover of this book depict a person or persons, such person or persons are merely models and are not intended to portray any character or characters featured in the book.

THE PROFESSOR'S DRAGON

It was love at first sight… with my professor. What's a dragon to do?

For two years, I've been pining over Professor Sarris. I knew the moment I saw him that we were meant for each other, but it's not to be. For one thing, I was his student, and he's the most ethical man I know. For another, he has no idea I'm actually a four-thousand-year-old dragon from another dimension.

When my people fled to Earth to avoid extinction, I vowed to clean up my life and stop acting like a fledgling. It's bad enough that nobody takes me seriously… sure, maybe I used to be flighty and irresponsible and caused a few interspecies incidents, but that's all in the past. I have big plans for the future, and this college gig is the first step in proving myself. I'm not endangering this fresh start for anyone.

But then my professor and I wind up at the same party, and suddenly it seems he's not completely out of reach. Except I'm still the adorable flirt nobody wants to rely on, and convincing him we should be together while proving I'm a changed dragon is a monumental task.

Good thing I'm up for the challenge.

PROLOGUE

Dustin

TWO YEARS AGO

THE GRIN on my face is so wide, I think I'm scaring my fellow students. My *fellow* students. That's right, I'm a student! Today is officially my first day of college, and I'm so excited, I might actually burst.

Just think, I am one of the first dragons ever to attend college… well, on Earth, that is. But we didn't have college like this back home—our education system was different. So it definitely counts.

It's been three years since we fled our home dimension for the sanctuary offered to us here on Earth, and in that time, we've been focusing on healing from the trauma of our loss and assimilating with Earth society. For the first time ever, my grandfather, who's the wing leader of all dragons, and King Raðulfr of the elves actually allowed me to have some responsibility. I've been an "unofficial" liaison between the government and the people, initially explaining what was going on and telling them about Earth and then later helping people get settled and gain access to support they needed. People like me, so it was easy for them to trust me and for me to help them. For the first time in nearly four thousand years, I finally got the chance to be useful, and it felt amazing.

It was also wonderful to see Grandfather's perception of me change. I've always had his love—he pretty much raised me, since both my parents died when I was just a fledgling—but I didn't feel like I had his respect. That might be partly my fault—there were a few incidents that weren't entirely trust-inspiring—but when Caolan convinced Grandfather and King Raðulfr to give me a shot as the civilian liaison, all that changed. And when the job wound down as people became more comfortable with our new home, Grandfather listened to me more. It took some convincing, but he finally agreed that college would be a good way for me and other interested dragons to learn more about Earth's history and society and interact with humans. So far, we've kept mingling with humans to a minimum, since giving away the fact that we exist would be catastrophic. The community of species here on Earth has been in hiding from humans for nine thousand years, living side by side with them but always being careful not to reveal that they're different. It would be really rude of us to accept their hospitality and then give away their secret within just a few years.

So while we've joined the greater community and mix with humans all the time during daily life, anything that would require prolonged exposure—like college—has been a no-go. There are very few dragons and elves even working with humans—since our numbers are so low, the Community of Species Government was able to help our people mostly find work with community-owned businesses. Those who have been allowed to work with humans are generally older, experienced, and highly trusted by my grandfather and the king.

Until today. Today, I take a new stride in dragon-human relations. Even if the humans don't know about it.

Speaking of, I'd better get moving. My first class is in a few minutes, and standing in the middle of campus grinning at people isn't going to get me there.

I set off in the direction of the lecture hall. I know exactly where I'm going—I came here a few times last week to familiarize myself with the campus. It's important that Grandfather continues to see me as a responsible adult, and not the flighty young problem I used to be. I wave and smile at a few people as I pass, because how else will I make friends? Some of them wave back, some look confused, and one gives me a downright nasty look. I guess not everyone's as socially adept as I am.

In the auditorium, I manage to get a seat in the front row. For some reason, it's still half empty, even though the rest of the seats are filling up fast. Maybe these seats are reserved? Nobody tells me to move, though, so I get out my laptop, ready to take notes. Whatever reason people have for not sitting at the front works in my favor. After three years, my English is good enough that I don't use the translator spell anymore, but some of the material for this course—Introduction to English Literature—dates back several hundred years and is in a slightly different version of English. My friend Alistair, who's a hellhound and has been a huuuuuge help in teaching me all the important Earth things, said it might be tricky to understand at first, so I want to be nice and close to the professor where I can hear clearly and see facial expressions for context. If that doesn't work, I can fall back on the translator spell, but I'd rather not. I want this to be as authentic an experience as possible.

Two men come in and stride to the front of the room. One is older, although not old. I still find it hard to judge the ages of Earth species, especially humans. There's a little bit of gray flecking through his hair, but his face is mostly unlined. He's beautiful. Like… my heart starts to beat faster, he's so beautiful. I squeeze my eyes shut, sure he must be some kind of hallucination. No living being can be that lovely.

But when I open them, he's still there. And the younger man with him—the… aide? Assistant? Alistair told me about them, but I don't remember what they're called—is handing out stapled papers. I take a stack, keep one for myself, and pass the rest behind me like the other people in the front row are doing, but my eyes keep going to the front of the room. Is this the professor? Can I be so fortunate that I'll be able to gaze upon his perfection twice a week all semester?

Can I be so cursed?

How will I be able to concentrate on the coursework and what he's actually saying if I'm entranced by his beauty?

He goes to stand at the lectern and taps the microphone, and the noise level in the room begins to subside. Students slide into seats, and there's a rustle of paper from those who prefer to take notes longhand. That's not me, since I've never actually learned how to write in English. I can read it, especially when it's typed, but actually forming the letters by hand isn't something I've taken the time to master.

"Welcome to Introduction to English Literature. I'm Professor Sarris. If you're suddenly realizing you're in the wrong place, now's your chance to leave. No hard feelings, I promise." He pauses, and I seize the chance to draw breath. His voice is just as beautiful as the rest of him… deep and sonorous, but with an edge of humor.

There's a small flurry of movement behind me, presumably as someone who is supposed to be in a different class leaves, but I don't bother to look. Why would I when there's such a visual feast right before my eyes?

"Okay, let's get started then. This is Marcus, my TA, who will be your point of contact for anything not directly related to the course material. You should all have a copy of the syllabus in front of you—put it away. If you haven't already read the online version, you can review it in your own time. Make sure you do—all your assignment due dates are in there. Does anyone have any questions about the syllabus?" He pauses again, and it takes me a moment to realize he's just asked a question. I'm so enjoying the sensation of his voice washing over me. He has a wonderful energy.

Fortunately, I have no questions about the syllabus— the online version was very clear—because I don't think I could string a coherent sentence together right now. I *want* to—oh, how I want to. I want his attention on me. His gaze locked with mine, that tiny quirk of a smile directed at me. To be the focus of all that intensity would surely be the pinnacle of my life.

Some fool in the back asks about extensions—extensions! We haven't even begun—and Professor Sarris patiently answers. I don't hear his exact words, too caught up in their cadence, but everyone laughs, so he must have said something funny. I smile, thrilled that I'm not the only one who can see how wonderful he is.

I pinch myself. This intense infatuation is beginning to get creepy and weird. Maybe I should have eaten more for breakfast this morning. Is my blood sugar low? Am I in fact having a hallucination right now? Maybe Professor Sarris is actually quite ordinary. Or even unattractive, with a strident, shrieky voice.

I cast a spell that draws energy from around me and converts it to the sustenance my body needs. We rarely use this spell anymore, since eating actual food is so much more fun. The spell doesn't have any flavor. It also barely tops me up, so I guess my energy levels are fine and I'm not experiencing a starvation-induced hallucination.

"No more questions?" Professor Sarris asks, gaze skimming the seats. "If you find you have some later, you can ask Marcus—or make an appointment during my office hours. Let's get started."

If I thought I had any hope of overcoming my insta-lust, it's dashed within the next few minutes. His passion for his subject matter and the clear excitement in his voice when someone asks a relevant question seal the deal for me. That's it. It's done. I'm head over heels in infatuation.

Sigh.

WITHIN WEEKS, my situation becomes dire. He's handsome. He has a lovely voice. His aura is beautiful. He's passionate about his chosen field. He's knowledge-able. He has a way of teaching that makes everyone in that huge lecture hall feel included. He's never scathing or rude, even when people say foolish things. He has this faint air of reserve that disappears when he's actually teaching, but instantly returns when class ends.

My infatuation has grown and changed. I'm now lost to my love for him.

It's damn annoying.

For one thing, I have to work twice as hard outside of class, because I can barely concentrate in it. He called on me for a question the other day, and I stuttered for a full twenty seconds before I managed to get out the wrong answer. And while I love him for the way he simply smiled kindly and said, "Not quite, but I love that you're so invested in side characters," I'd really rather be able to be myself. I've never stuttered over a man in my life, not even my first crush when I was a fledgling. Confidence is something I have in spades. Walking up to strangers and flirting is something I've been doing since I was old enough to have sexual urges.

That's how I know this must be love. It's different. It's debilitating. I hate it.

But I love him so.

In the meantime, people are noticing. Zara, who's my new best human friend and is in a few of my classes, has already guessed I "have a crush," as she calls it. One of the guys in our discussion group flat-out asked me how I can be so good at talking about the book with them but turn into a "gibbering idiot" in class. He got elbowed hard by the girl who's always with him and shushed by some others. Zara told me later that they all think I have some kind of social anxiety that causes problems in large groups. I didn't even know what social anxiety was until then—I had to look it up. I really hope none of those people are in any of my other classes, where I have absolutely zero problem speaking in front of hundreds of people, or they're going to get suspicious. The last thing I need is for a rumor to start about my unrequited love.

Because of course it's unrequited. If I had any inkling my feelings could be returned, I would throw myself at him… possibly naked. I talked to Alistair about this, and he's pushing for me to do it, but how can I take such a risk? This isn't just a hot man I want to fuck. I *love* him. Far better to bask in his presence and admire him from afar than to risk having him transfer me to another class. Although the sex would be nice. Being in love with someone who doesn't love me back means I'm in a bit of a dry spell.

Alistair says that's even more reason to fuck him, but it doesn't feel right to me. It's very odd, since I've never before attached any kind of emotion to sex. Well, not beyond vague fondness and appreciation. This concept of sexual fidelity to someone who barely knows I exist is disturbing and weird and very, very frustrating. After listening to me whine for ten minutes, Zara suggested I buy a Fleshlight and download a video of one of Professor Sarris's lectures. Nobody seems to understand the hell I'm in.

If this is love, I don't want it.

Wait… I really do.

"I THINK I'm going to like college," Fabian says, smiling and twiddling his fingers at a group of frat boys. "My, they're awfully fit, aren't they?"

I roll my eyes. Fabian is even more sexually confident than I am—or than I was, I should say. The last two years have been a big change for me. I can't bring myself to fuck anyone other than my love, and since he's unavailable, it's just been me, my Fleshlight, and the assortment of other toys I've invested in. I tried picking someone up for a few hours of fun, but I ended up crying and babbling to him about my unrequited love. Luckily, he was really nice about it, made me a cup of hot chocolate, and let me talk for hours. We still meet for coffee sometimes. I introduced him to his current boyfriend, and they're talking about moving in together. So... you know. Silver linings.

"Come on. The cafeteria is this way," I tell him. As a junior, I'm familiar with almost every building on campus, even the ones I've never had classes in, because

I have friends everywhere. I'm a friendly person. People like me. *Why* has my love never noticed me that way?

Anyway… where was I? Oh, yes. I've taken it upon myself to show Fabian around, now that he's decided to take some classes. He's our historian and record keeper, and he's heard me talking about the impact of literature and art on Earth's cultural history enough to become interested in learning more. He was especially intrigued by what I told him about Earth's study of philosophy. We dragons are quite renowned for being philosophers —it goes hand in hand with an unrestricted lifespan and being literally created from energy—but the Earth approach is very different. I'm taking one of the same classes as Fabian this semester just to see him argue with the professor.

"Dustin!"

I turn toward the familiar voice, and Zara waves. A moment later, she joins us. "Hey. You going to get some food? I'm starving." She smiles at Fabian. "I'm Zara."

"This is my cousin Fabian," I introduce quickly. It's not true, but we decided it was a good way to forestall any questions. As we've slowly begun socializing more with humans, we've noticed that they have a kind of sixth sense that we're not exactly like them. Of course, they don't have the imagination to guess the truth, but I've often been asked if I'm related to someone they've met before. They seem to be treating the sense of "otherness" as a physical resemblance, even if there isn't one at all.

Fabian and I also live in the same house, so this covers all bases—even if we never invite humans to come there.

"Nice to meet you." Zara glances at me. "Dustin's mentioned you before."

That's true. I've talked about my "family" a lot. It's hard not to when I live with them.

"I'm his favorite cousin," Fabian claims immediately, even as I shake my head. He grins at Zara. "He's talked about you too. You're his second-favorite person at college."

We push through the doors to the cafeteria as Zara laughs. "Oh? Who's his favorite?" She side-eyes me. "Or need I ask?"

"We're not talking about this," I insist and try to ignore them as they discuss my pain as though it was an entertaining soap opera. We get food and manage to find three seats at a table by the window.

"My good-luck charm." Zara reaches out to ruffle my hair, and I duck her hand as I drop into a chair. "Dustin has the best luck at finding tables. Every time I'm with him, we find seats."

I avoid Fabian's sardonic look. He knows very well that I cast a spell encouraging the people sitting here chatting to move along.

What? It's not like they were still eating. They can talk outside in the fresh air instead of hogging a table.

Fortunately, that distracted them both from snickering over my love life—or lack thereof. We talk about our class schedules, about what Fabian thinks of the campus, about what we did over the summer. Fabian and I are careful to only share limited details—it wouldn't be good if we mentioned that we both spent some time in the Pamir mountains, teaching summer courses to the fledglings at the flight school.

"...incredibly fun," Zara is saying about the

skydiving course she took, when a faint tingle of my senses tells me my love is nearby. This has happened a few times over the past two years—I'll get this warm, melty feeling and every nerve-ending in my body perks up. It had literally never happened in my life until I met Professor Sarris, which gives even more credence to the theory that this is love.

Whatever. I focus intently on my burger. I am *not* turning around. This year is going to be different. Love will not rule me.

"Dustin," Zara hisses, "he's *here*."

"Who?" I bluff, even though we've been through this before many times, and we both know I know who. Sure enough, she gives me a dark look.

"Yeah, who?" Fabian asks, and oh no. He may know about my deep pain and unrequited love, but I never thought he'd actually be in the same room as Professor Sarris. I clearly didn't think things through before I told him he'd love college.

"No one." I try not to sound desperate, but from the way Fabian's eyes widen, I've failed miserably.

"Is it *him*?" he whispers, leaning forward, then looking around eagerly.

"I don't know what you're talking about." Sweat rolls down my spine. We dragons can regulate our own body temperatures, so it's not because I'm hot.

"Where is he?" Fabian asks Zara, who gives me a sideways sympathetic look.

Then betrays me.

"See that tall guy there? The one in the blue blazer with the glasses?"

Fabian blinks a few times. "That's him? Wait, are we

talking about the same subject? That's the guy Dustin is in love with?"

"Yep." Zara sits back and picks up her Coke. "He's been pining and making an ass of himself in class for two years."

"No longer," I declare. "Thank fuck that's over, at least."

She raises both eyebrows in surprise. "You're not in love anymore? No more pining?"

Heaving a sigh, I shake my head. "Sadly, that seems like it's going to continue. But since I'm done with all his classes, there won't be any more of me acting like an idiot."

"Hang on, wait," Fabian interrupts before Zara can make a snarky comment about me always being an idiot. "*That's* the man you love? Turn around and look. I want to be sure there's no misunderstanding."

"I was in two of his classes," Zara points out dryly, "both with Dustin. I'm pretty sure I wouldn't make a mistake about this."

Fabian shakes his head. "I just can't… Dustin, look. Please?" He gives me big, pleading eyes and pouts.

With another huge sigh, I brace myself and half turn in my seat to peer through the crowd, even though I *know* he's here. I can *feel* him. And sure enough, there he is, smiling politely at the student dishing up pasta for him. My heart does its usual stutter at the sight of him, and my lips curl up slightly. It's been months since I've laid eyes on him, not since school let out last year, and I hadn't realized how much I needed this. The nagging feeling in my gut eases.

This could be a problem. I'd hoped that not being in any of his classes this year would help, that not having to see him so often would allow my feelings to slowly fade away. But instead, it seems I'm just going to miss him.

Tearing my gaze away, I force myself to turn back to Fabian. "Blue blazer, glasses, getting pasta," I confirm. Part of me wishes I'd never told him about my feelings, but that first semester, I was so swept up in them, I couldn't help myself. Besides, I was struggling so much with concentrating in class that I really needed Percy's help, and once one person in our house knows something, everyone does. There's no such thing as a secret at Here Be Dragons.

That's the name of the estate, by the way. Catchy, right?

"B-But," Fabian stammers, "you said the man you loved was an incredible beauty. You said he shone with it! That one glance at him was enough to render the heavens dumbstruck!"

"Say what?" Zara asks.

I narrow my eyes at both of them. "What's that supposed to mean?"

They exchange a glance.

"Look, Dustin," Zara begins in a conciliatory tone, "don't get us wrong. The subject of your undying love has definitely got that whole hot professor vibe going on. But I wouldn't say he shines with beauty. Or whatever that was about the heavens."

I sniff. "Clearly you're mistaken. Maybe you don't see it because you're a lesbian."

She screws up her face in a way that says that's not it, but concedes, "Maybe."

"Well, I'm not a lesbian," Fabian declares loudly—too loudly. Conversation at the tables closest to us stops, and people look over at us. "I am decidedly gay, and I am an expert on all things cock-related, including male beauty."

"Oh my god," Zara mutters, sliding down in her seat as sniggers erupt. The sorority girls at the next table break into applause.

"You go, honey!" one of them calls.

Fabian looks around in confusion. "Go where? What?"

"She's encouraging you," I explain. "Because you just announced to half the room that you love cock and are an expert on it."

"Oh." He appears to think about it, then shrugs. "No lie there." Waving at the sorority girls, he calls back, "Thank you!"

They seem delighted, and he turns back to us smiling. "Where was I?"

Zara looks at me dazedly. "Do you remember when I said you were kind of weird but I liked you anyway?"

I nod. "Sure. It was right after we realized we were in all the same classes in first semester."

"And you said you were the normal one in your family?"

"Yep."

"And I laughed and said I didn't believe you?"

I smirk. "Told you so."

"Excuse me, are you saying *Dustin* is more normal than I am? Because that's patently untrue. I am an *expert* on social norms in our culture, and by any definition—"

I cut in before he slips up and says something to give away how our culture is from another dimension, has wings, and can breathe fire. "What were you saying before? When you found it necessary to tell the world that you're not a lesbian?"

He frowns. One thing about Fabian that you can bet money on is that it's easy to distract him as long as you're asking a question. He really is a fount of information and an expert in about a million different things, and he loves to share his knowledge.

"We were talking about Dustin's professor," Zara reminds him, gesturing to where my love is now sitting at a table across the room, and I bite my lip, wishing he really was *my* professor.

"Oh! Yes. I was saying that as a non-lesbian cock expert, I can assure you that while your professor is attractive, the heavens aren't dumbstruck by his beauty."

He's kidding, right? I turn again to look across the room at Professor Sarris. As always, I'm bowled over by how good-looking he is. How can Fabian not see it?

"Maybe you just need glasses," I suggest, even though I know it can't be true. We're beings of energy. Our bodies don't fail like that.

"Or maybe love has addled your brain," he counters. "Having lived with you both before and after you fell in love, I'm inclined to think that's the right answer."

"Percy and Grandfather are in love, and their brains aren't addled."

"True," Fabian concedes. "But it might just be you."

"Your family dinners must be wild," Zara observes. "Fabian's probably right. This is just a case of rose-colored glasses."

We both snap our mouths shut. I've heard that expression before, but I'm not entirely sure I understand it, and a glance at Fabian shows he's in a similar boat.

"Maybe," I say noncommittally. We'll ask Percy later. "Whatever it is, it doesn't matter. He's beyond my reach."

"Is he, though?" Zara asks. "I get why you didn't want to do anything while you were taking his classes, but now that you're not… why not take a shot?"

"Yeah," Fabian echoes, his face alight with delight. "Why not? I can help!"

Zara squints at him. "How, exactly, would you help? Never mind." She holds up a hand. "I think some things it's better I don't know. But I would like to know if you're going to, uh…" She hesitates for a moment. "… to fight for your love." There's a faint tremor on the last few words, as though the mere thought has her overcome by emotion.

She's such a good friend.

Then she bursts out laughing. "I'm sorry, I'm sorry," she cries. "I'm not laughing at you, I swear!"

Fabian looks around, frowning. "Who are you laughing at, then?"

"She's laughing at me," I tell him. "Only not in a mean way. It's more that she's laughing at the situation."

He shakes his head. "I don't get it. You're in love with someone who you think barely knows you exist, and you're not willing to fight for your love. How is that funny?"

"It's not," Zara gasps between chuckles. "But that language—fight for your love. That's fucking hysterical! I don't know how you can say it with a straight face. Is your whole family this dramatic?"

Fabian and I look at each other. We're not dramatic. Are we?

Fortunately, before either of us have to come up with an answer, she continues, "Don't let me get distracted. I want to know if you're going to do anything about your unrequited love now that he's not your teacher anymore."

I bite my lip, and she makes a noise of annoyance.

"How do you manage to do that and pout at the same time? It shouldn't be possible! You're like… super twink."

Super twink! Yessssss. "Do I get a costume? Something with glitter," I muse, thinking about it. Alistair would probably be able to help me with that. He has a real flair for costumes.

"Gahhh… we're getting off topic again!" Zara reaches out and pinches me.

"Ow! What was that for?" I make a show of rubbing it like I've seen her and other humans do, but thanks to a quick spell that boosts healing, the pain has already faded.

"Answer my question, or I'll pinch you again. And I'll keep pinching you every time we get distracted."

"I really like you," Fabian tells her. "Can you be my friend too?"

She beams at him. "Sure. You seem like a good person. Why don't we— Ugh, it happened again!"

This time, when she reaches over to pinch me, I pull my arm out of the way. Just because I can dispel the pain quickly doesn't mean it's something I want to experience again.

"Stop it, Zara—I'll answer!"

They both stare at me expectantly while I try to get my thoughts in order. How to explain this? I've never in my life been afraid to ask for what I want. I've never hesitated to flirt with anybody who caught my interest. If you don't try, you won't succeed, right?

But this is different. If he says no…

"Dustin, I swear—"

"I'm afraid," I blurt. "What if he says no?"

Zara's expression immediately morphs to one of sympathy, and this time when she reaches out, it's to pat my arm, not pinch it. Whew. "Aw, honey. That would suck, but the thing is… nothing would change."

I blink.

"Think about it," she continues. "Right now, you're loving him from afar and there's no relationship between you, right?"

I nod warily. I can see where she's going with this, and I don't like it.

"If you walk over there right now—or go to his office later, or catch him somewhere on campus, or whatever—and proposition him and he says no? You'll be right back to loving him from afar with no relationship between you."

"Maybe, but—"

"*But*," she interrupts, holding up a finger. Fabian's gaze fixes on that finger as though it holds the answers to all life's mysteries. "What if you proposition him and he says yes?"

"That would be amazing," I confess as images rise in my mind's eye. Me and Professor Sarris cuddling on the couch, us laughing together, us walking hand in hand… us naked and writhing against each other. I shove the images aside. "The thing is… I don't think he'll say yes." My chest physically aches as I force those words out, and Zara draws back as though in shock. Even Fabian seems surprised.

I make myself go on. "Think about it. He might not

be *my* teacher anymore, but he's still a teacher at this school, and the school doesn't allow relationships between teachers and undergrads. He might not be willing to risk his career and reputation. He might not be interested in a relationship with someone who's, uh, so much younger." I cast Fabian a stern glare. The reality might be the other way around, but Zara can't know that. "Or he might not even be interested in men. Or blonds. Or he might be married or otherwise involved. There's way more chance of him saying no than yes."

Zara's nodding sympathetically, but Fabian shakes his head. "So? There's still a chance he'll say yes, right? The Dustin I know has never hesitated to leap in even when the odds were dire."

I hate him. The first thing I'm going to do when I get home is ask Kethe to make fish for dinner. He *hates* fish. It would serve him right.

To my surprise, Zara comes to my rescue. "I get it," she says. "With the odds so much against you, it's better to hold on to the sliver of hope that maybe it *could* happen, rather than take the risk and find out it definitely won't."

I point at her. "What she said," I tell Fabian.

He looks doubtful but shrugs. "I don't understand love, I guess. I've always considered one fuck as good as another."

"What I feel for him is not about fucking," I declare passionately, then reconsider. "Well… not *just* about fucking, anyway. There's some fucking involved—quite a bit, really—but there's also feelings. Lots of feelings." I sigh and let myself turn to look across the cafeteria at Professor Sarris. "Beautiful feelings."

"Sounds uncomfortable," Fabian says. "I think I'll stick to fucking."

If only.

CHAPTER TWO

Rob

"Your admirer is staring at you again," Gerald, who works with me in the English department, says somewhat gleefully. "I'm so glad he's back this year. I was worried he'd graduate or drop out and I wouldn't get to see him moping around after you anymore."

I want to ignore him, but I can't quite keep myself from defending "my admirer," as he puts it.

"Don't be snide. He doesn't mope." I stab my fork into my pasta just a tiny bit harder than is necessary. Not for the first time, I wish I had never shared any information with Gerald. But when he pointed out one day, nearly two years ago, that there was a student staring at me, I'd thought it safe enough to mention that he was in one of my classes and seemed to have a crush on me.

Big mistake. Huge. I haven't heard the end of it since. It doesn't help the matter that Dustin's really not subtle.

"What's this?" Kelly, who's new to the department, asks. Gerald volunteered to show her around and help her get familiar with everything when she first started, and now he's helping her get to know the rest of us—which is the reason for this lunch, when I could be having a perfectly good sandwich in my office while reading.

"One of the students has a thing for Rob," Gerald says. "He's been mo— Er..." He catches my sharp glance. "...admiring him for two years."

"Oh, that poor kid," Kelly says, which raises my estimation of her quite a bit. "I'm guessing he's been in your classes? Does he make things awkward?"

I shake my head, because honestly, part of me has been wishing Dustin would just say something. At least then I could have gently let him down and arranged for him to work with another professor for anything that required one-on-one meetings.

That's the only reason I wish he'd say something, of course. No other reason.

Yeah, no one's going to believe that. It's an outright lie. Not that I'd ever do anything that could be seen as abusing my position of authority over a student... but he won't be my student this semester. I checked. And doesn't that just say it all?

"He's never done anything inappropriate," I tell Kelly. "Mostly he stares, then blushes if I catch him. He used to get really flustered if I called on him, so I stopped doing that. My TA and the rest of the department have informed me that he's suitably loquacious when I'm not around, so I guess I make him nervous."

"He's a good student," Gerald admits, almost grudgingly. "Very bright, quick to understand, always participates—you can rely on him to put his hand up when the rest are feeling shy. And he helps anyone who asks for it. From what I've heard, he's popular with everyone but… I don't want to say he's unaware. He's not clueless about his self-worth. But more that he just accepts it as normal and doesn't let it inflate his ego?" He shrugs. "I don't know. But the only time I've ever seen him speechless and self-conscious was when I stuck my head into one of Rob's lectures."

"Has he been in many of your classes?" Kelly asks.

"Three. One when he was a freshman, and two last year."

She winces. "That must have been tough for him. Do you have him again this year?"

I shake my head, and Gerald smirks. "Checked already, did you?"

Crap. I should have just said I don't know. Because yes, I checked, but they don't need to know that. "I don't think so," I prevaricate, but from the way Gerald laughs, it's too little, too late.

"So he's not your student anymore," he muses, glancing back across the cafeteria to where Dustin is sitting with two others. One has also been a student of mine, but I don't know her name offhand. I do know that she and Dustin are quite good friends, since she's with him a lot of the time. The other man, I don't recognize at all.

"Wherever you're going with that, don't." I'm perfectly aware of the school's rules regarding faculty and undergrads. Dustin's not my student anymore, so there would be no real conflict, but it's still against the rules and still not a step I'd be willing to take. Especially with him being more than twenty years younger than me. Based on something I heard last year, I think he still lives at home—he needs to experience life independently before entering the kind of adult relationship I would expect.

Although a one-nighter is incredibly tempting.

Gerald looks like he wants to say more but doesn't, and Kelly graciously changes the subject.

I concentrate really hard on not looking over at the adorable blond twink who's on my mind far too much.

MY CELL PHONE rings while I'm preparing dinner that evening, and I know it's my mother without looking. She left a message yesterday that I haven't got around to returning yet, which means she's convinced I'm either dead or have been kidnapped by sex traffickers. It doesn't matter how often I tell her that sex traffickers aren't usually interested in forty-five-year-old English professors who are going gray and soft around the middle, she maintains it's a valid concern.

"Hey, Mom," I answer, bracing myself.

"Robbie! How *could* you? Not even a text message to let me know I didn't have to call the police. I've been worried sick! I barely slept a wink last night."

I'm not really a horrible person who worries his mother. She sleeps like the dead every single night. It's a particular gift of hers—no matter what's going on, the minute her head hits the pillow, she's out for eight hours.

"I'm sorry, Mom. Classes are starting, and things have been a bit crazy."

She sniffs, and I grin. My mom is one of the most amazing people I know, but she has a real flair for drama. My stepfather thinks she must have been a hellhound in a previous life. That's not an insult—well, not really. Hellhounds aren't really evil minions of hell. They're just canine shifters with a weird sense of humor that led to them changing their species name.

Yes, that's right—shifters exist. Cool, huh? When I was seven and Mom met Julian, I thought he was just a really nice guy who recognized how awesome my mom is. Then things got serious between them, and we found out he's actually an incubus—a being who feeds on sexual energy—and that there's a whole community of other species living side by side with us humans that we don't know about. Shifters, vampires, demons (also not the hell kind), and of course incubi and succubae. Mom's marriage welcomed us into the community of species, and I was thrilled and fascinated by it. That's what ultimately led to my choice of careers—when you get the chance to actually talk to people who lived at the same time as Dickens and Shakespeare and even Chaucer and hear about how the literature of the times did and didn't represent their actual lives… it's mind-blowing.

Don't even get me started on everything that happened five years ago when elves and dragons from another dimension fled here to Earth for sanctuary. I still can't quite get my head around it, but I've met a few elves since then, and if I were a cultural anthropologist, those meetings would have been the best moments of my life. Their history must be incredible.

Mom starts telling me about all the things going on in her life. Julian is a very wealthy—like "Rob, that Ming vase in the entrance hall is not to be used as a goalpost" kind of wealthy—former industrialist, and by that I mean he was in on the ground floor during the industrial revolution. About twenty years ago he turned all his businesses over to his kids—all of whom are more than fifty years older than me but still look younger—and got involved in charity instead. Mom was thrilled, and now the two of them spend their time actively fundraising for various good works.

"…haven't forgotten the party Saturday night, have you?" Mom demands as I turn off the heat under the wok.

"I haven't forgotten," I promise dutifully. She and Julian don't invite me to all their fundraisers, but every once in a while she likes me to attend so she can "show off her college professor son." It's sweet that she's so proud of me, and she usually only invites me to parties where there will be a lot of community members, which I like. Even after nearly forty years, I'm still crap at picking them out of a crowd, and I would *never* risk exposing them by approaching a random person on the street who *might* be part of the community, so the only time I can talk to a vampire or whoever is when I'm at one of Mom and Julian's parties. "I'll definitely be there."

"Wonderful! Julian has a meeting at CSG later this week, and he's going to invite the lucifer and some others. It should be a great night."

We chat for a while longer while I eat. Mom's of the opinion that if we were eating together, we'd converse during our meal, so there's no reason why we can't converse over the phone while eating. I'm not about to argue with her. She asks me about my class schedule for this year and reminisces fondly about her own college days, which she does every year at about this time. Thankfully, she no longer includes any of the wilder stories. There are some things a man just doesn't need to think of his mother doing.

My meal is done by the time we end the call, so I clean up the kitchen and then pull out my laptop to finish making some notes for tomorrow's lecture. The material is pretty much the same as last year, but there's always a fresh angle to use, and some of the reading I did over the summer gave me an idea of a way to intrigue more students. The general ed classes usually have a lot of bored new adults with no interest at all in literature, and I've been told more than once that I should let someone more junior within the department teach them—I have the seniority to pick and choose which classes I want. But I see it as my chance to see what people really think of literature and find ways to change their minds. It's arrogant of me, but hey, I'm not hurting anyone.

It's not that late when I pack up and go to bed. As I slide between the cool, clean sheets and close my eyes, I let my mind wander back over the events of the day. Dustin's face rises in my mind's eye, and my breathing hitches. I've been teaching for twenty years, and I've never been tempted by a student before, not even when I was only a few years older than them. There's always been an invisible line in my mind that acted as a barrier to any attraction. I even wondered how others who have crossed that line could be so stupid and lacking in restraint.

But I get it now. I'm still determined not to act on this attraction, but I understand why someone else might have. If Dustin were to give me any indication he wanted more from me… well, it might prove impossible to resist.

My mental image of him takes on a life of its own, one sparkling hazel eye winking at me while his cheeks pinken with a blush, and I slide my hand into my sleep pants and wrap it around my erection. This doesn't break any rules, at least. Just as well, because it might be my only solace for a while.

CHAPTER THREE

Dustin

IT TAKES Fabian less than a day to find his feet on campus. I'm not surprised—he and I are a lot alike in that sense. Neither of us is shy or afraid to try new things. By Thursday, I'm only seeing him on the drive to and from school—and at home, of course.

I hate that drive. It's only forty-five minutes, and the car is a nice one, but being closed into a box for any length of time is uncomfortable for us—especially since we could fly the distance in just a few minutes. But there's nowhere close to campus that's absolutely safe for us to land and shift back, what with all the students wandering around at all hours, so it's not an option. Making the drive every day is still better than the other option, which is living on campus and not having any opportunity to shift.

Don't get me wrong—I love my biped form. There are a lot of things I can do in this form that I can't do as a dragon… like sex. But our natural form is as a dragon, and we tend to get antsy if we can't shift back regularly. Kind of like wearing tight clothing for a whole day. Toward the end, you just can't wait to get out of it.

Today, Grandfather has requested that I join him at the office in the city for a meeting with the team that handles community outreach. I'm so chuffed—this is what I've wanted for so long, for him to see me as someone who can make a valid and useful contribution. The people on the outreach team are all highly skilled and great at their job, so it's unlikely I'll do more than smile and agree with their plans, but it's great to know that Grandfather is so happy with the job I did as civilian liaison that he wants my opinion on this. It gives me hope that when I finish putting together the plan for the project I've been thinking about, he'll let me run with it.

Fabian decides to come with me so he can talk to some of the archivists at CSG about the crossover between community history and what he's learning in his human history classes. It's only been a few days, but already he's super excited about all the research opportunities college is going to give him. He's such a geek.

The college is in a midsize town between the city and our home—though closer to home—so it takes not quite two hours to get to the office. Fortunately, Grandfather arranged to lease a few secure parking spots for our use, so we don't have to waste time looking. Tonight we'll stay in the condos Grandfather and his people use during the week while they're here rather than going back to Here Be Dragons. It's going to make for an earlier start tomorrow morning, but Fabian and I are both early risers anyway.

We make it to the office with fifteen minutes to spare before the meeting, and I wave to Fabian as I get off the elevator. He's going upstairs to the CSG floors. I come to an abrupt halt in the reception area—Grandfather and the king are there, along with Sam, the current lucifer, and David, his right-hand sorcerer, talking to an incubus I don't recognize.

I wander over to the reception desk, where Dáithí reigns supreme, and ask, "Am I late?" I'm sure I'm not, but maybe things got moved around and I just didn't get the message.

He shakes his head. "The lucifer and David brought him down to meet the king and Brandt. They said not to bother with finding a meeting room, since they're not staying." He pointedly glances at his watch and raises his voice. "That was ten minutes ago."

Sam, a felid shifter with exceptional hearing, laughs, and Grandfather rolls his eyes.

"Okay, Dáithí, we'll stop cluttering up your reception in just a few minutes," he says. I grin at Dáithí and then go to join the group.

"Good afternoon, everyone," I declare. "It's good to see you again," I say to Sam and David. I spent a lot of time with them when I first came to Earth as part of the advance team, and we bonded over plans to thwart supervillains and impending doom.

"You too, Dustin," Sam says, smiling at me. "You should come see us more often."

"I will," I assure him. "I've been busy with college."

"And painting the town red?" David asks pointedly, and I cough.

"That was one time, and it was Alistair's idea. How was I to know he didn't mean it literally?"

He grins—which always surprises me, since he's usually very no-nonsense—and reaches out to pat me on the shoulder. "I'll tell Caolan you're here. Don't be surprised when he comes to find you." His boyfriend is one of King Raðulfr's closest advisors and one of my favorite people. He was the one who convinced Grandfather and the king to give me some responsibility. I'll always be grateful that he believed in me.

"I'll look forward to it," I promise, then turn my attention to the stranger and offer my hand. "Hello. I'm Dustin."

He shakes my hand with an amused smile. "It's lovely to meet you, Prince Dustin," he says warmly. "I'm Julian Harlow. I manage several charities that I'm trying to convince the government to promote."

"Just Dustin," I correct him. Technically, being the wing leader's grandson does make me an honorary prince, but we dragons don't really go in for formality all that much. When you live as long as we do, it starts to seem kind of silly. "What kind of charities?"

We talk for a few minutes about the programs he's running and the ones he wants to implement. We're both concerned about the lack of funding for youth services in rural and regional areas. There's some cross-over between some programs he wants to tackle and my future plans, so I'm able to make suggestions based on the research I've done. He seems impressed.

"You're a very impressive young man," he compliments me, and I chuckle.

"Julian, I mean this in the nicest way possible, but I'm probably older than your recorded family ancestry."

"Dustin," Grandfather chides, but he's smiling. It's true, after all. These Earth species don't live as long as we do—I think the oldest recorded person was about fifteen hundred years.

Julian is chucking too and shaking his head ruefully. "It's going to take me a while to get used to that," he concedes. "You have the manner of a young man still, but I should know better. Tell me, do you have plans for Saturday night? My wife and I are hosting a fundraiser, and we'd very much like to see you there. I think your insights would be valuable in convincing people to part with their money."

Pride explodes inside me, but I make myself hide it, maintaining the same smile of low-key amusement. Someone else who recognizes that I have something to contribute! Although… he might just be sucking up to Grandfather and the others, who've already shown how fond they are of me.

Still, it's another chance to prove my worth.

I flick a glance at Grandfather, who nods slightly, letting me know it's fine. I wouldn't want to do anything to interfere with his official standpoint—there was enough of that when I was younger.

"Thank you, I'd like that," I say graciously, and Julian beams.

"Excellent! Well, I won't take up any more of your time—I know you weren't expecting me." He takes his leave, and Sam and David go with him after reminding me to visit them. I'll go upstairs to the CSG offices after I'm finished here.

"Dustin," the king says to me, "you are a revelation."

I blink. "I… am?"

"You are. I never thought this day would come, but I'm so glad to be wrong. I think you're going to be an excellent statesman."

"I agree," Grandfather says, putting an arm around my shoulders and turning me in the direction of the meeting rooms while I try to regain my wits. "Now let's move, before we're late."

This might just be the best day ever.

JULIAN and his wife are holding the fundraiser at their home in the city, which at first led me to believe it would be a small event. As I get out of the car and look up at the mansion in front of me, I'm forced to reassess.

"Wow."

"Big, right?" Steffen says, coming to stand beside me. As the head of security for grandfather and all dragons, he gets invited to all these events. It's a small problem, since Steffen is a paranoid conspiracy theorist and has likely already come up with several potential threats posed by this location that don't exist in reality. I already promised Grandfather and Percy that I'd keep an eye on him. He's really very good at his job, but he can be overzealous at times, and we don't need him tackling someone at a posh party just because they glanced in Grandfather's direction for too long.

"Very big. There are going to be more people here than I expected."

"It should be a good night, though," Percy tells us, taking my arm and tugging me forward. "Julian and his wife are excellent hosts. Oh, just so you know, his wife is human."

"Really?" I know some humans have been integrated into the community—my friend Noah is one of them—but they're quite rare. "How does that usually work? Do they wait until the relationship is very serious

before revealing the truth? If I was in a serious relationship—"

"Which you never have been," Steffen interrupts.

I roll my eyes. "No, but if I *was*, I'd be pissed way the
hell off to find out my significant other was keeping such
a huge secret from me."

"But it's not something that can be revealed early
on," Stef argues. "Otherwise there would be millions of
humans who know the truth."

Seriously, talking to him is exhausting sometimes. "I
know that. I'm just saying, it's not an easy situation, and
I'm not sure how it would work."

"Fortunately," Grandfather interjects, "we can ask
Percy."

We all look at Percy, who sighs. "Really? We're going
to do this on the doorstep?"

We wait.

"Fine. Usually it's just a matter of hoping the human
is enough in love to understand and forgive the need for
secret keeping. Most do, once the situation has been
fully explained. There are also some situations where the
human was already aware before entering the relationship—usually because they have a family member or
very close friend who's already part of the community.
Cross-species fertility is very low, but it exists, so there
are some community members with a human parent
and siblings." He reaches up and straightens Grandfather's collar. "Now, do you think we can go inside?"

Steffen half raises his hand. "I have some
questions."

"Can they wait until later?"

He shakes his head. "Not all of them."

"Are they about potential conspiracy theories?"

Grandfather asks, and Steffen lowers his hand. "Nobody here is going to harm us, Stef. I promise."

"Definitely not," Percy assures him. "They want us to donate money now and in the future. If anything, they'll go out of their way to make sure we're safe and happy."

Stef squints, and I'm pretty sure he's just come up with some new theories that involve a long-term plot to lull us into complacency, so I take the initiative and start walking up the steps to the front door.

"That settles that, then. Let's go in."

I can hear Stef grumbling, but they follow me anyway.

A man in a black suit opens the door just before I reach it. "Good evening," he says. "May I have your name?"

Oooh, this is exciting! There's another man a few steps behind him and to the side, holding a clipboard and wearing a headset. I've never been to a party like this.

"Dustin Draco," I announce. Draco is the surname most dragons use—since we got to Earth and discovered we'd need a surname to blend in with the humans. There are only about five thousand dragons, so it's not like the planet was suddenly overrun with Dracos. And some did opt to pick their own unique names.

I turn to Grandfather and Percy. "Are all the parties and fundraisers you come to like this? With the fancy security? If I'd known, I might have come along sooner." This is like a movie.

The man at the door clears his throat, but when I turn back, his face is just as politely bland as before. The other guy is smiling, though, and I give him a wink.

What? Just because I have no interest in casual sex anymore doesn't mean I can't flirt. It's like breathing.

"Thank you, Mr. Draco," the first man says. "And the rest of your party?" He glances over my shoulder, then does a double take. "Lucifer! Er, I mean Mr. Caraway." He shakes his head ruefully. "My apologies, sir."

"Not to worry," Percy says lightly, stepping forward with a smile and that soothing air that makes everyone relax. Really, it's like he's a walking, talking prescription for anxiety medication. Being around him just makes you feel better.

"It's good to see you, sir." It's been nearly five years since Percy was lucifer, and everyone seems to like Sam, but Percy still gets this reaction everywhere he goes. It's nice.

The man's eyes move to Grandfather. "And this must be Wing Leader Brandt."

Since they seem to have it all under control, I slip past man one and sidle over to man two. "Hi."

He gazes down at me, his eyes lingering on my forehead—probably because I'm not using glamor and we dragons have different bone structure from the Earth species. Now that I'm not peering at him through the doorway, I can see the horns that denote he's a demon. No wonder he's so big. And I managed to get a smile out of him! It's gone now, but believe me, getting a demon to smile isn't always an easy thing. Most of them are pretty dour.

He doesn't greet me in return, but I don't let that stop me. "I'm Dustin. I really like your muscles. They look great in that black suit."

Blinking, he says, "Uh… thank you." He looks over my head toward the door, as if his friend can help him.

Pffft.

Batting my eyelashes at him, I say, "The first person from Earth I ever met is a demon, and now I have a soft spot for them. A big, handsome demon like you is a magnet for me. Do you get a break later? We could talk. I could tell you all about dragons." I actually mean exactly what I'm saying—not interested in casual sex right now, remember? Plus, I'm here as a diplomatic envoy of sorts. But I love making new friends, and he *is* a big, handsome demon.

Who's just started stuttering.

"Dustin, leave him alone," Percy says, wrapping an arm around me and steering me onward. I glance back over my shoulder and wriggle my fingers in a wave goodbye. My new demon friend just shakes his head, but he's smiling. Score for me.

We enter what appears to be a large sitting room. The design is very clever—there's a wall of doors opening out to a patio, and the room flows through an archway into another, creating quite a large entertaining space. Not as large as some of the rooms at Here Be Dragons, but then, that's a country house and somewhat bigger. I feel an exhilarated tingle run through me—anticipation, perhaps.

"Percy, Brandt!"

We look to the left as our host joins us, accompanied by a beautifully dressed attractive older woman. I'm still not good at guessing human ages, but I'd put her in her sixties. Right now, she and Julian seem to be at equivalent stages of their lifespans. I assume she's been taught the human variation of magic and is either already using the life spell or will start soon.

I file that away to ask Percy later. It's definitely not something I want to bring up now and risk a social faux pas.

"We're so glad you could join us," Julian is saying warmly. "This is Erika, my wife and other half. Darling, you know Percy, but meet Wing Leader Brandt and Prince Dustin."

I wince. He seems to have forgotten to be informal.

Grandfather and Erika shake hands and exchange pleasantries, and then she turns to me and holds out her hand.

I take it and smile at her from under my lashes. I'm adorable, and I know it. Older women *love* me. "It's just Dustin," I tell her. "May I call you Erika? I don't like to be formal with beautiful women."

Just as I expect, she laughs. "Oh, I like you, but I'll bet you cause more than your share of trouble."

Grandfather sighs. "He certainly used to."

"I'm reformed," I assure her, even as I feel a jolt of pleasure at the way Grandfather phrased his words.

She looks me up and down. "Normally, I'd say you're far too young to be reformed from anything, but I'm guessing you're older than you look."

I put a hand to my chest. "Are you asking me to reveal my age?" Leaning in, I whisper, "I could have changed your husband's diapers… but if anyone asks, I don't look a day over thirty."

She laughs again. "You don't look a day over *twenty*, you cheeky thing. But since you're not twenty, there's someone I'd like you to meet." She half turns and gestures across the room, then looks back at me. "You're single, aren't you, darling? Because I think you'd be perfect for my son, but I draw the line at breaking up happy couples."

"I'm single," I assure her, "but I'm not looking to change that." I hesitate, then add, "My heart is taken." It's not something I usually tell strangers, but I really like her—my instincts are all telling me I can trust her. There's a special kinship between us.

Her smile fades, and she pats my arm. "Oh, honey. Is there any chance we can convince your heart's owner to claim it?"

I shake my head.

She nods. "Well, you'll just have to get over them, then. And what better way than by getting under someone new?"

Percy snorts. "I'd forgotten how much fun you are, Erika."

Erika waves a hand. "I do my best. Now, Dustin, you *are* into men, right? I don't want to get my son's hopes up only to find out you're straight."

"He's into men," Percy assures her, and I side-eye him. Whose side is he on?

She claps. "Wonderful! And here's the man I want you to meet." She reaches off to the side, just out of my line of vision. A strange shiver goes down my spine as I half turn toward the newcomer and—

Freeze.

My throat closes over, and I make a sound that has Percy exclaiming in concern and Grandfather demanding, "Dustin, are you okay?"

Holding up a hand to forestall their worry, I cough lightly to clear my airway and croak, "I'm fine. Sorry.

Uh… swallowed wrong." I cough again, then lift my eyes to meet the gaze of my one true love.

He looks incredible in formal clothes, with his hair brushed back… and he's definitely surprised to see me.

Erika pats me lightly on the back, then says, "Prince Dustin, I'd like you to meet my son, Robert Sarris. Rob is an English professor at Beresford University."

Behind me, Grandfather and Percy suck in a sharp breath. They're not stupid. They know exactly what's happening here.

"*Prince* Dustin?" he sounds shocked. Erika frowns.

"Yes. Dustin is the grandson of Wing Leader Brandt… who I'll introduce you to next. Don't be rude, Rob."

He seems to shake himself. "My apologies. It's just that I know Dustin. He's been in some of my classes. I didn't realize you were a dragon, Dustin."

He. Knows. Who. I. Am.

He recognizes me. *Remembers* me.

Someone's sharp finger jabbing into my spine jerks me out of my stupor. Right. Talk. Words. "Uh, yes. Dragon. Me. Hi."

"Oh dear," Percy murmurs, then comes to stand beside me. "Good evening—Rob, right? I think we've met before. I'm Percy Caraway."

Professor—er, *Rob* tears his gaze away from mine and takes Percy's hand. "Yes, I remember. It's good to see you again. I hope you've settled well into your post-lucifer life."

"It's been delightful. Let me introduce you to Brandt, whose mission it is to keep it that way."

Grandfather joins us and eyes Rob up and down. "So

you're Dustin's professor," he says, and I want to die a thousand deaths. Maybe Rob will think he's just referring to him being one of my professors, rather than *my* professor.

"It seems so," Rob says with a charming smile. "It's good to meet you, sir. I have so many questions about dragons."

"Dustin can answer those for you!" Percy announces.

"I'm sure Dustin can fill you in!" Erika proclaims.

They look at each other and smile conspiratorially, and I want to—

Wait a second.

Wait just one second.

He's not my teacher anymore.

His mother is trying to set us up, which means he likes men and is single.

He knows I'm a dragon, not just a twenty-year-old human.

Maybe… maybe it's time to take a chance.

But what if I do and he's not interested? My hopes will be dashed forevermore.

I need a sign. A sign from him that he finds me attractive.

I smile, shoving aside all my nerves and seizing the opportunity. "Of course I can tell… er… may I call you Rob? Or should I stick to 'Professor'?" I add a rueful little chuckle. I don't want to seem too flirty right away. I need to ease him in.

Sure enough, his expression softens. "Rob is fine. After all, I'm not your teacher anymore."

There's something almost tortured about the way he says it, but all I can focus on is the fact that he noticed.

He noticed I'm not in his classes. That's gotta be a good first step, right?

"Great! Why don't you show me where to get a drink, and we can talk all things dragon? I'm *very* knowledgeable. I've had four thousand years to learn things." Yes, I drop that in there deliberately. Just in case he's wondering if I'm a very young dragon.

He breathes in deep through his nose, and a slight wash of color stains his cheeks. Another good step.

I lean over and kiss Erika's cheek. After all, if things go well, she's going to be family. "Come and find me later. I'm not done getting to know you."

"Oh, you charmer!" She grabs me in a quick hug. "We're going to be the best of friends."

Winking at her, I screw up all my courage and slide my arm around Rob's. He starts but doesn't pull away.

"Grandfather, Percy, I'm going to chat with Rob for a bit. Make sure you're on your best behavior while I'm gone."

Percy chuckles, but Grandfather's gaze is slightly worried, and I'm overcome by a rush of love for him. He raised me, and the one thing I've never doubted is how much he loves me—even when he was vowing that I was the most exhausting, troublesome creature to ever live, his first concern was that I was unharmed.

"We'll keep them out of trouble," Julian assures me with a grin, and I look up at Rob.

"Drink?"

He gives himself a little shake. "Yes, of course. It's this way." He leads me through the room to where a wet bar is set up in the corner. I concentrate on my steps and breathing evenly, even though I think my whole right side might be numb from being in contact with his body.

Don't get your hopes up. Be cool. Look for a sign.

I've got this.

The bartender gets our drinks, and then we drift away from the bar toward the doors to the patio.

"It's such a nice night," I say as we step outside. "I have to admit, though, it's still weird to look up and see your sky."

That shakes him out of whatever thoughts were putting a frown on his face. "Really? Did you not have a sky… or was it just very different?"

I try not to let the pang of sadness take over. After all, I'm the one who brought it up. "A bit of both. The stars were all different, of course, and then as the collapse of the dimension progressed, they began disappearing, changing the night sky even more. And the last two thousand years, our atmosphere was so damaged that we didn't have a clear view anyway." I scan the sky above. Even with the light pollution from the city around us, the stars are still visible. It's nice.

He clears his throat. "I'm so sorry for what you—all of you—have had to go through. I'm glad things worked out so you could come here." He sounds stilted, which is so unlike the confident, passionate man I'm used to seeing. Of course, he's used to seeing me as a stammering mess, so we're both full of surprises tonight.

"Thank you. It's been an adjustment for most of us, but Earth is beautiful and we love having so many new peoples to get to know. We dragons are very curious, you know."

"Really? So that's not a myth? There are so many things they say about dragons. For so long, we thought they were just stories, and now it's hard to unravel the truth from the rest."

I pat his arm and let my hand linger. "Well, anything connected to castles in the Middle Ages and sacrificial virgins is made up. There were none of us here then. But we are curious, and we do keep hoards." That's one of the things I get asked most often from my Earth friends in the know. Also, I'm leading him in a very clear direction.

His face lights up. "You have a hoard? May I ask what's in it?"

I smile at him and stroke my hand along his arm. "Kisses."

For a moment, he just stares in confusion, then his expression closes over. "If you prefer not to tell me, that's fine. I don't want to be rude."

I laugh and lean against him, loving the way color creeps up from his collar. "No, I'm telling you. I hoard kisses. There's a spell—it's for children, really. Parents use it at bedtime, or when they have to be separated from hatchlings who might miss them. It corporealizes a kiss into something they can hold on to or keep on their pillow—a reminder that they're loved."

His lips part slightly. "Really?" he breathes. "That's wonderful." Then he squints slightly. "Why do I get the feeling you're not collecting parental kisses?"

I pat his chest lightly—and then leave my hand there. "You know me so well already," I tease. "I *do* have some kisses from my grandfather and my parents. I managed to bring those with me when we migrated. But most of my hoard got left behind, so I've been trying to rebuild it. It's not a sexual thing, though I do have a few from former sexual partners." From before I stopped having sex with other people. "Most of what I have now is friendship kisses."

"Friendship kisses?" He seems somewhat skeptical, but I'm completely serious.

"Yes. Look—kiss me. Just on the cheek. I'll show you."

He looks around. "Uh…"

"Nobody's paying attention, and honestly, nobody who knows me will be surprised. People kiss me all the time. I'm adorable. I kissed your mom before, and no one even blinked." I stop and snort. "Wow, that sentence is fucked-up."

"The part where you kissed my mom, or where you claimed to be adorable?" he asks dryly, but he's grinning now.

I arch an eyebrow and pout. "It's not just a claim. Look at me!" I step back and do a twirl. "The word 'adorable' was invented with me in mind."

He laughs outright. "I can't argue with that."

"Right?" I step toward him and lean in, trying to ignore the butterflies swarming in my stomach. *This is it.* "So kiss me."

He hesitates, then leans down and pecks me awkwardly on the cheek. I release the spell at just the right moment to capture the sentiment in the kiss. When he draws back, it flutters between us, yellow verging into orange, which means he's a little uncertain but hopeful.

"See?" I say, holding out my hand, palm up, for the kiss to settle onto.

"It can *fly*?" he gasps. "Is it sentient?"

I shake my head. "No. And it's not really flying. The energy of the emotions in the kiss let it flutter around a bit, but that's all. That's also why it's so small—because that kiss was barely a kiss." I frown up at him from beneath my lashes. That's proved a very effective weapon for me in the past.

Robert clears his throat. "Well… so every time anyone kisses you, you collect it?"

"Not every time. It has to be a kiss from someone I want to remember." His breath hitches, and color rises on his cheekbones. I restrain my glee and continue, "If it's going to be in my hoard, I'll be seeing it for millennia to come. I don't want to keep one from the creepy guy who kissed me before I could turn away on the dance floor at a club."

He frowns, and I hurry on.

"But friends and family and people I like? Sure. My friend Sophie, who lives at the estate with us, gives me a kiss every morning just because she knows I hoard them. Those are lovely memories. And I have some from people I've dated—those relationships might have ended, but there are still some good feelings to remember."

There's a thoughtful look on his face, and I decide to increase the pressure a bit. "Do you want to give me a proper kiss now? Something that would be bigger than half a Tic Tac?"

A chuckle bursts from him. "Half a Tic Tac, huh?" He studies the kiss on my palm. "That seems about right. Okay, why not?"

Don't tell, but I'm surprised it worked.

I angle my cheek toward him. I could offer him my lips, but this isn't about stealing intimacies he doesn't want to give. This is about building trust and showing him I'm not just his student.

I swear it is.

So when his lips touch my cheek, that's all I'm after.

I release the spell and expect him to draw back right away, which is why I'm already moving... I swear, I wasn't expecting him to linger. Wasn't expecting our mouths to brush together.

Or for fireworks to explode.

In my head, of course. And maybe a little bit in my pants—not a literal explosion, since we dragons don't do that, but soldier Dustin definitely stirs to life.

Is it just me, or is Rob still lingering?

He jerks back, and the magic passes.

"I'm sorry," he stammers. "I didn't mean—"

"It's fine," I assure him. "An accident. A very happy one, but no reason for concern. And look." I point to our second kiss, which is fluttering alongside the first one. This one is much bigger and the colors flow from yellow through orange and into a deep rose pink, the color of sexual passion.

That's a sign, right? He's definitely interested.

"It's beautiful," he admits. "Still, I overstepped. I shouldn't have done that."

Okay. Time to be bold. "Why?" I ask. "We're both adults. Me much more than you, by the way."

Startlement crosses his face, as though he'd forgotten that I'm much, much, *much* older than him.

"Uh... yes. But I'm your teacher."

"Not anymore."

His breath hitches, and his gaze darkens. "I-It's still... not..." The words fade away as he swallows hard. I say nothing, just look up at him, lips slightly parted, trying not to hyperventilate from the joy of being this close to him.

He lowers his head and captures my mouth with his. *Yes!*

It's a thousand times better than the accidental kiss before, because this time he means it. He wants it. And he's putting a whole lot of passion into it.

Passion I'm more than happy to return.

I wrap my arms around his neck, and it's only the fact that he crushes me close that stops me from wrapping my legs around his waist. There has never been anything better than this—my whole body is alive, tingling from head to toe, and my magic is rushing through me. I feel more powerful, more confident, more *me* than I ever have before.

"Well," an amused voice says, "this isn't quite what I expected you to teach my son about dragons."

For a second, I hope that Rob somehow didn't hear. That hope is dashed when he breaks our kiss. We stare at each other, panting, and then he turns his head toward his mom, letting me go.

"It was… I shouldn't have… I apologize." He lets go of me and steps back, hands coming up to steady me when I stumble—deliberately—then falling away again when he's sure I'm steady. "Excuse me." He turns and moves away, but his mother grabs his arm.

"Don't be an idiot, Rob. You've done nothing wrong." She glances over at me. "Has he?"

I shake my head. "Absolutely nothing. Unless you count walking away."

Erika grins at me approvingly, then looks at her son. "See? Now why don't you and Dustin keep on getting to know each other? You could go to my study upstairs—it should be nice and private."

Wow. Did Rob's mom just…?

"*Mother*," he hisses. I guess she did. I don't know how I feel about that.

Well… if he takes me upstairs, I'll feel grateful. Sadly, it doesn't look like that's going to happen.

Sure enough, he shakes his head, mumbles another apology, and rushes into the house. I sigh.

Erika turns to face me. "I'm sure him running away is no reflection on that kiss," she offers, and I smirk.

"Oh, trust me, it definitely wasn't." If I'd had the mental capacity to cast a spell while he was kissing me, that last one would have been a huge, vibrant red and purple mass of energy. I've had a lot of kisses in my life, good and bad, and that blew out the top of the meter.

"I don't know why he's being so stubborn," she frets, turning her head to glance after him. "I'd really like to see him settled and happy. He spends far too much of his time on work. Even most of his friends, he met through work. He needs someone to shake him up." She glances at me hopefully.

Looks like I have Erika firmly on my side. Good thing, since she'll be my mother-in-law.

"I'm the perfect person to shake him and then settle him down," I assure her. "Don't worry. He's still processing the fact that I'm not a naïve twenty-year-old. He'll come around."

Now that I know he's interested, there's nothing to hold me back. The fear and self-consciousness have dropped away, and my old self settles in.

He wants me. I want him. This is something I can work with.

CHAPTER FOUR

Rob

I SMILE and wave at people I know as I pass through the house but don't stop, then hurry up the stairs and lock myself in one of the guest bedrooms, leaning back against the door.

Fuck. Me.

Sucking in a deep breath, I move through the dim room to the attached bathroom, flip the light switch, and blink as the bright light bounces off the white tile walls.

Fuck.

I run cold water and splash it over my face. Part of me is reluctant to wash the taste of Dustin off my lips, but I know I won't be able to function if I don't.

How can my life have been upended so quickly?

Turning off the tap, I stare at myself in the mirror, water dripping down my face and off the end of my nose. I'm kind of surprised by how normal I look. How can anything be normal after that kiss?

Oh my god, that kiss.

Instinctive guilt kicks in my chest, and I remind myself that Dustin's not the kid with minimal life experience that I thought he was. He's also not my student anymore.

Although he is still a student at the college. That's a line I've never crossed, and even if I'm not—seriously not—in any position of authority over him—he's a fucking *dragon*, for fuck's sake—I'm still not sure I want to cross it.

Holy fuck, I kissed a thousands-of-years-old dragon. How many thousands? I'm sure he said, but I can barely maintain my train of thought right now, much less remember things. And what a kiss. Is that just because he's a dragon? Like, do they have some kind of kissing mojo, similar to what incubi can do?

Or is it because I was kissing Dustin? Do we have a kind of special chemistry that I've never experienced in my life before?

Groaning, I grab the hand towel from the rail and mop up my face. "What do I do now?" I ask my reflection.

It doesn't answer, the bastard.

Okay. So I kissed Dustin. So it was the best kiss I've ever experienced in my life. So what? That doesn't mean it has to lead anywhere.

Or maybe I should just be patient. He's a junior this year, right? So only two years until he graduates and is no longer a student at the college where I work. Two years isn't long—especially not in the lifespan of a dragon. And I have a social connection to him now. I can wait two years, pretending he's just another kid on campus, and then when he's graduated, I can ask Mom to invite me to a party he's at and make my move.

If he's still single. I mean, an adorable, sexy, intelligent man like that? Someone smarter than me is bound to snap him up. Someone who's not a middle-aged human with a penchant for books and minimal social life.

Also, if I tell Mom this plan, she'll laugh in my face. It's pretty obvious that she loves the idea of me and Dustin together—what with the matchmaking and the suggestion that we sneak off to a private room—and she's not going to take kindly to being told it's on hold.

Sighing, I tidy up the bathroom and then lean on the black granite counter. This evening has been a big shock —just learning that one of my students is a dragon is trippy. Seeing him in his natural form, without the glamor to make him look "human," only intensified my attraction to him. The fact that he's chasing me in earnest and I want to be caught, despite my ethical qualms… there has to be a solution.

But there isn't one. Either I compromise my morals and ethics… or I let Dustin go.

The memory of the kiss rises to the forefront of my mind.

How do I let that go?

I'm jerked out of my moody introspection by a knock on the guest room door. "Rob?"

Damn. I should have known Mom wasn't going to quit. Resigned to my fate, I leave the bathroom and am halfway to the door when Mom opens it, apparently sick of waiting.

"Rude," I chide. "What happened to waiting until you were invited in?"

She waves dismissively. "Old people get some leeway on manners," she jokes, flipping on the light. "Why are you skulking in the dark?"

I go back to the bathroom and turn off the light,

then join her in the armchairs by the window. "I am not 'skulking.' And you're not old," I add, and she huffs.

"Thank you. That took you a little too long to say, my boy."

"Don't fish for compliments with me, old woman," I tease. This kind of banter is normal for us, but I'm also hoping it will distract her from talking about Dustin. It's a futile hope, but nobody said hope had to be worthwhile.

Her piercing look proves that I know her too well. "What was that about downstairs?"

"I already apologized," I remind her. "It won't happen again."

She rolls her eyes. "That is *not* what I meant, and you know it. Come on, hurry up and tell me—I need to get back to my guests."

"Please do," I invite, beginning to stand. "I'll join you." There's no point in hiding up here. I can avoid one-on-one time with Dustin just as well downstairs— there have to be at least a hundred people here.

"Sit," she orders, and I might be a grown man, but I indulge her anyway… making sure to sigh as if I'm making a huge sacrifice. "Why are you afraid of Dustin?"

What? I stare at her. "Afraid? I'm not afraid. Have you seen him? Dragon or not, he's the least threatening person alive. There are kittens less adorable than him."

"Afraid *emotionally*."

"Mom, have you been drinking?" It's a desperate, last-ditch effort to get out of this conversation, but she just levels me with her mom stare. The one that always makes me feel like I've done something I need to apologize for. I resist the urge to beg for forgiveness.

"Fine," I concede, but then assert, "I'm not 'emotionally afraid.'" I'm not giving in on that. "But he's a student at the college, and it would be unethical—not to mention against the rules—for me to get involved with him. I crossed a line tonight that makes me ashamed of myself."

Her expression instantly changes to one of concern. "Darling, you did nothing to be ashamed of. Surely you can see that these are very special circumstances? Dustin is hardly a naïve child just venturing out from under the care of his parents. Julian says he was instrumental in the migration effort, and he was very impressed by the conversation they had the other day."

"I get that," I agree. "You forget, he's been my student—in several classes. I'm well aware of how intelligent he is. And thoughtful," I add. "Popular too. But he's still a student, and since there's no way to explain the situation to the school, any… any…" I don't want to say "relationship," because we basically just met and it feels like jumping the gun, but what else can I call it? "…interaction we have would need to be secret. And that just feels wrong to me on so many levels. I don't want to be dating someone I can't be with publicly."

She sighs, then purses her lips. "I suppose I can understand that," she concedes. "Although I'm begging you, never use 'interaction' in that context again."

I snort. "Believe me, I won't." This time when I stand, she doesn't stop me. I offer a hand to help her up, and she takes advantage of it to launch herself into my arms.

"I only want to see you happy, darling. I love you so," she says, hugging me fiercely, and I'm swamped with a wave of love for her. My mom might not always be conventional, and she might be a dramatic busybody determined to arrange my life, but she's been the best mom I could ask for, even when it was hard. People judged her for being an unwed mother, she had to work two jobs to put food on the table while studying part-time to finish her degree, and she had to choose between her convictions (calling our landlord scum and setting fire to his car) and keeping us housed. We did plan exactly how that car fire would go, though, right down to our getaway route to Canada. Julian's entry into our lives might have eased the financial hardship and chased off the scummy men who thought they could take advantage, but it never changed how fiercely and totally in my corner she was.

"Love you too, Mom. And I am happy."

She pulls back and gives me a look of pure disbelief. I don't bother to argue, just escort her back downstairs to the party.

And spend the next few hours trying to avoid Dustin.

It's not easy. He's *everywhere*. And whatever shyness he was suffering from in my classes is clearly gone. His flirting is so obvious that other people begin to notice, and soon any attempt I make to maintain distance between us is thwarted by my mother's guests.

Everyone wants to be a matchmaker, it seems.

Finally, I sidle up beside Julian. "Save me," I murmur, "or I'm leaving right now without saying goodbye to Mom."

He casts me a sidelong glance, amusement writ large on his face. "I don't know why you don't just succumb. You make a very attractive couple… and just think of all the research he could save you."

"You think I should hook up with him because he'd save me time on research?" I thought incubi were supposed to be the more sensible members of the community. That's what Julian's been telling me for nearly forty years, anyway. I guess sensible means something different to them.

Julian shrugs. "That and the fact that you're both lusting after each other so badly, it's arousing half the people in this room."

My gut turns to ice. "Really?" How humiliating. I skim my gaze over the people nearby. I'd forgotten—yet again—how sensitive a sense of smell most of them have. Hellhounds most of all, but all community species have stronger senses than humans—and of course, incubi and succubae feed off sexual energy, which includes lust. They're all just usually so polite about not mentioning that they know.

Like when I was a teenager and first started beating off. I thought I was being very sneaky about it but didn't account for the fact that Julian could literally sense the sexual energy that resulted from my self-care. About a week after I discovered my new favorite hobby, he sat me down and gave me "the talk." I found out later that it took him a week to get to it because he needed to research human puberty and sexual health first. And when I protested, avoiding his gaze and with a hot face, that I didn't need to know all that stuff, he laughed and said, "You can get away with telling your mom that, but my senses are a little sharper. You don't need to be embarrassed about it—sex is a natural part of being an adult. I just want you to be safe. We never have to talk about it again after this if you don't want to."

So… yeah. There's no keeping sexual secrets with this lot.

Julian takes pity on me. "Come on, this way."

I follow him without paying attention to where we're going, one eye on the crowd in case Dustin pops out. He's proven to have a gift for appearing as if from nowhere.

"Here we go," Julian announces. "He's not likely to want to flirt with you here."

Smiling with relief, I look up… at Dustin's grandfather. I swear, my smile vanishes so fast, my facial muscles actually ache from the speed of the movement. I cast an acidic glance at my wicked stepfather. He smiles sunnily back at me.

"Thank you," I murmur, not wanting to say anything that might offend the men in front of me. "Hello again. Have you been enjoying your evening?"

Percy Caraway, who was lucifer for longer than I've been alive and only retired about five years ago, smiles at me. It's a polite expression, but I can see the laughter dancing in his eyes. He knows exactly what his step-grandson has been up to, and it amuses him greatly.

Great. So glad I can entertain.

Wing Leader Brandt, on the other hand, is scowling at me, his eyes narrowed. "Have you been leading my grandson on for the past few years?" he demands, and I feel Julian stiffen beside me.

"Brandt," Percy says sharply. It's not quite a snap but definitely conveys his displeasure. "This is Dustin's business, not yours."

Brandt sucks in a deep breath through his nose, nostrils flaring, his glare fixed on me… then sighs and rolls his eyes like a teenager. "*Fine.* Do you at least like the theater? I don't think Dustin should be with anyone who's not appreciative of the arts."

What, exactly, am I supposed to say right now? Do I start with "I'm not planning to be with Dustin"? Or defend my appreciation of the arts?

Aware that my mouth is hanging open and probably makes me look like a dying fish, I manage, "I've never led Dustin on. He was my student. That's all."

"We know," Percy assures me, and Brandt finally smiles. It's wide and toothy and somehow manages to be draconian even though he doesn't shift form.

"Dustin has been very forthcoming about you… although not with your name," he grumps. "We're well aware that the silver in your hair glints when it catches the light, and that your voice deepens when you get passionate about what you're saying."

A wave of heat flows up my neck and into my face. I guess if I'd had any doubt about Dustin's crush, it would now be dispelled. Beside me, Julian is making choking sounds as he tries not to laugh.

It's so nice to have the support of a loving family.

Discreetly, I step on his foot.

"So we're completely aware that you've been nothing but professional with him," Brandt continues.

It takes me a moment to catch up, and I frown, confused.

"So asking me was… what, a test?"

Brandt nods. "You passed, in case you're interested."

Victory zings through me, and I have to firmly remind myself that I am *not*, in fact, interested in passing any tests Brandt might require for me to date Dustin. Because I won't be dating Dustin.

I really won't.

At least, not for the next two years.

Maybe after that, if he's willing to forgive me then for smashing his hopes now.

Hey, who knows? He might be cool with it. For a person as old as he is, two years is nothing, right? After all, he's been crushing on me for that long without getting bored of it.

"Dustin is a student at the school where I teach," I remind Brandt—and myself. "A relationship between us would be completely inappropriate."

All three of my companions laugh.

"Oh, you're serious," Percy says with some surprise. "Ah… well, that's very commendable of you, but you have to realize this isn't an ordinary situation and Dustin certainly isn't in the same category as your other students. He's only at college as a kind of social experiment."

"You'd be surprised how many of my students are only at college as a social experiment," I say dryly, thinking back over the years and all the students who thought the English department was an "easy" way to get a degree.

"But they were still very new adults," Brandt says. "Dustin is certainly not that, even if I do still think of him as a fledgling."

It strikes me suddenly that if Dustin is thousands of years old and looks like he's barely old enough to drink, then his grandfather could be *much* older.

Very much.

Enough that several thousand still seems like a child.

My curiosity is piqued, but I would never do something as rude as ask a person's age. Maybe Julian knows and can tell me later.

"It's still a situation that would make me uncomfortable," I say firmly, just as the back of my neck prickles. Without understanding why, I turn my head…

…and my gaze clashes with Dustin's across the room. He smiles slowly, his eyes bright, and my chest rises and falls with a sigh.

Why does he have to be so pretty? And sweet… intelligent…

How am I supposed to resist him?

"I think uncomfortable is something you'll need to learn to live with," Percy commiserates, and I tear my gaze from Dustin, who's making his way toward us.

"I'm sorry?"

Percy tilts his head in the direction of the blond flirt who's taken over my evening. "I'm just saying, you might intellectually be determined to resist, but your heart and body are singing a different tune." His nose twitches slightly, and the wave of embarrassed heat is back. Oh *god*, they can smell my response to Dustin.

His grandfather is literally sensing my lust for the man he thinks of as a child.

I don't think I've ever been this humiliated before, not even the time in high school when I ripped my pants in the cafeteria on a day I was wearing a *very* brief jockstrap.

Fortunately, Dustin reaches us before I can respond —and isn't that a change of heart? Until this second, I would have said I was determined to avoid Dustin for the rest of the night, but it seems the need for a distraction is more important than anything else.

"Hi!" he says cheerfully, then smiles just for me and bats his eyelashes. I've read what feels like a thousand books that describe characters as batting their eyelashes, and every single time I marveled over how stupid they must have looked. Maybe they did, but Dustin definitely does not, and I swallow hard as my cock stirs slightly.

"Rob?"

This is ridiculous. I'm a grown man in my midforties. Fluttering eyelashes shouldn't be able to get me hard.

"Rob?"

Even if he does have the prettiest eyes I've ever seen.

"Rob!"

I start, then frown at Julian. "There's no need to shout."

Percy clears his throat, but Brandt laughs outright.

Shaking his head, Julian says—with a great deal of exasperation—"I'm going to get a drink. Would you like one?"

"Uh, no. Thank you. I've had enough." I need to keep a clear head, what with Dustin hovering at my elbow, gazing up at me adoringly. It would be really easy to get swept away by that and do something stupid.

"You're so responsible," Dustin coos, laying a hand on my chest and leaning in. "There's nothing quite like a responsible man."

So much for Julian's theory that he wouldn't flirt with me in front of his grandfather.

Casting a rather desperate glance at Brandt—who seems to be both amused and irritated—I take a small step back, trying to extricate myself without seeming rude. Or hurting Dustin's feelings. Because I don't want to do that.

He steps with me. So much for that idea.

In fact, he seems to be closer now. If I breathe deeply enough, we might touch.

Do not *breathe deeply.*

"Uh," I mumble, unable to stand the awkward silence. "Not really that responsible. Just… uh."

He beams up at me and licks his lips. My gaze is immediately drawn to his mouth. So full and soft and pink and tasted better than anything ever in my life.

"But you are," he insists. "Responsible and clever and passionate… and so very hot." His fingers slide gently back and forth across my chest, catching on a nipple, and it's all I can do not to groan out loud.

Then he slides them into the gap between my shirt buttons and brushes against my bare skin. His fingertips feel like brands—only the kind that send currents of lust charging through me.

"Oooh, chest hair," he murmurs, looking directly into my eyes. "I've been wondering if you had any. I like a bit of fur on my men."

Oh god.

Clearing my throat, I grab his hand and pull it away from my chest. He pouts for a second, that delicious lower lip taunting me with how biteable it is, and then his smile is back.

"Why, Professor, if I'd known you wanted to hold hands, I would have offered."

I drop his hand like it's a hot coal, and the pout comes back.

I'm not going to survive this.

"Dustin," Percy says gently, "I think you're making Rob uncomfortable. Maybe ease up a little until he's had time to process this."

Those big hazel eyes gaze guilelessly up at me. "Do you need time to process? I can give you time. How much do you need? Five minutes? An hour? Two hours?"

"Two *years*," I exclaim, the words torn from me. I totally wasn't planning to say them. "Uh… I mean… you've been thinking about this for two years. I think I should get the same amount of time."

His jaw drops. "*Two years?* Are you crazy?" The smooth seducer is suddenly gone, replaced by… I don't know. He plants his hands on his hips and lifts his chin, sassy and stubborn and almost more irresistible with this facet of his personality coming out. "We are not waiting another two years to be together. You're just going to have to process faster."

I clench my teeth to keep from agreeing. Two years. It has to be two years. He needs to have graduated.

"This is the best entertainment I've had in a long time," Brandt says conversationally. "Dustin, I feel compelled to remind you that compromise is important. Remember we talked about that when you were small?"

"Not now, Grandfather," he snaps. "I'm busy. You're not serious about this two years crap, are you?" he asks me.

I nod, afraid to speak in case I accidentally tell him to come home with me now.

He stamps his foot and shakes his head. "That's not acceptable to me. Two hours, I was willing to give. Two years is too long." Suddenly the pout is back, and he catches my hand in his, gazing up at me pleadingly. "Please? Can't we just get to know each other better?" His thumb brushes back and forth over the back of my hand. "I just want to spend some time with you."

I'm mesmerized by him. "Okay," I find myself agreeing, and his whole face lights up with such joy, I can't even regret it. But when he attempts to throw himself into my arms, I catch hold of him and keep him at arm's length. "With conditions," I warn.

He draws back and narrows his eyes. "What conditions?"

It's very wrong that I want to kiss his sulky little mouth right now.

"No kissing," I insist. Mostly I'm warning myself, but it also works as a condition.

"No kissing?" he cries, then seems to catch himself. "Okay. I can work with that."

Oh hell no. "No sex or sexual contact," I continue, and he scowls. "In fact, no physical contact at all."

"At *all*?" he protests. "I'm a touchy-feely person. How are we supposed to get to know each other if I'm constantly on guard so I don't break your stupid rules?"

"Conditions, not rules," I correct, and I guess dragons aren't capable of setting people on fire with their eyes, because if they could, I'd be ashes right now. I relax a little. It's actually kind of fun, getting Dustin all riled up. And I can't deny that I'm excited about being able to spend more time with him… in a purely platonic and appropriate way, of course.

"Conditions, rules… it's all the same if I'm too busy worrying about them to actually get to know you."

He has a point. I might be hoping to turn this into a friendship that could eventually—in two years—become more, but that won't happen if he can't be himself. And I don't want to chase him away, even if that would be the sensible option.

"Fine," I concede. "Physical contact is permitted. But," I hurry to add when his wicked smile returns, "only the kind that would be appropriate if we barely knew each other."

"That's fine," he assures me.

"Barely knew each other as professor and student," I continue, because let's face it, there's a lot you can do with someone you barely know. Grindr isn't so successful because people spend weeks getting to know each other before having sex.

He heaves a sigh. "Fiiiiiiine."

I clear my throat to keep from laughing. He's so delightfully adorable. "Until I say otherwise, any time we spend together needs to be in a group environment."

"*What?*"

"Parties like this are good."

"They certainly are *not*," he exclaims, then turns to Julian, who's just rejoined us, and says, "That's not to say this isn't a lovely party, because it is. But it's not an ideal situation in which to get to know the love of my life better." The last few words come out between gritted teeth.

Did I say this was kind of fun? I was wrong. It's definitely fun, and I'm very much enjoying myself.

Wait. Wait.

Did he…

No.

CHAPTER FIVE

Rob

"Did you just call me the love of your life?" I ask. Surely he didn't.

He throws up his hands in exasperation. "What did you think this was all about?" he demands.

I don't know how to answer.

His expression morphs to incredulity and then rage. "Did you think I was going to all this effort just for *sex*?" He crosses his arms and glares. "I can get sex anytime I want, fuck you very much." His voice is rising, and the people in the group nearest us glance over curiously. "I wouldn't want to spend time getting to know you just for sex."

"How can you love me if you don't know me?"

"Why don't we spend time together and find out?" he challenges.

"As entertaining as this is," Percy interjects calmly, and we both look at him, "I don't think you're making much headway. Why doesn't Rob come to lunch tomorrow at Here Be Dragons, and you can continue this conversation afterward?" He turns to me. "There's a houseful of extremely nosy dragons in residence, so there's no chance of the kind of privacy that could lead to inappropriate things. They'd sniff that out immediately."

That sounds ideal for my purposes. I look at Dustin. "Is that acceptable to you?"

He sniffs. "I suppose. But we exchange phone numbers tonight."

I hesitate, because normally I don't share my cell number with students. They have my email, my office number, and can chat with me through the school site—which I have an app for on my phone, anyway.

"If you're not going to take this seriously," he begins, and I whip out my phone.

"I'm taking it seriously," I assure him.

He grants me a smile, then pulls out his own phone, unlocks it, and holds it out to me.

"Dustin!" a voice exclaims in horror. "What are you *doing*?"

Dustin groans and rolls his eyes while I look around for the newcomer. He appears as if from nowhere behind Brandt, then walks around him to join us and snatch Dustin's phone from his hand.

"You don't just hand a stranger your unlocked phone," he scolds. "Do you know what he could do with that? Next thing you know, assassins are breaking into your bedroom and you're fleeing into the night with a large-bosomed blond woman who has the secret formula they think you stole because he ripped off your identity!"

I blink. What?

"Ooh, that's a good one," Brandt enthuses, then

glances at Percy. "There were, what, two movies in that?"

Percy squints. "Three, I think. I particularly liked the mention of the large-bosomed blond. Tell me, Steffen, was she scantily clad? And perhaps wearing heels totally inappropriate for fleeing from assassins?"

The stranger—Steffen—sniffs. "Mock all you want, but these things happen." He waves Dustin's phone. "And it starts with being overly trusting of strangers. Next thing you know, he's going to agree to carry a nice old lady's bag through airport security and get arrested for trafficking drugs."

Dustin snatches his phone back. "That was one time. Please stop embarrassing me."

What?

"Wait… you really got arrested for trafficking drugs?"

"I was just about to ask that," Percy says, turning to Brandt. "I don't believe I've heard this story."

Brandt shrugs. "Airport security already suspected the woman and were actually watching her the whole time. They only detained Dustin for a short time to make sure he wasn't part of some kind of elaborate decoy plot."

"They gave me a very stern warning afterward," Dustin says with a sigh.

"And then you went home with one of them and didn't reappear for three days," Steffen adds, and I clench my teeth to hold back the snarl that wants to erupt.

"Steffen," Percy warns with a sidelong glance at me. "Perhaps you could refrain from discussing Dustin's personal business?"

Steffen looks confused. "Dustin's never been shy before." He looks at Dustin. "Why are you suddenly shy? Is someone threatening you? Blink once if you need assistance. I can help you."

Dustin covers his eyes with one hand, and I'm pretty sure it's only partly in embarrassed exasperation. The other part is so he doesn't accidentally blink and cause his friend to begin a rescue operation.

Aside from the whole Dustin-with-other-men thing, I'm enjoying myself.

"I'm not threatened," Dustin says through gritted teeth, then drops his hand. "Stef, have you been paying attention *at all* tonight?"

"Of course I have," Steffen snaps, offended. "I've been watching for signs of illicit incursion *and* keeping an eye on the suspicious characters."

"Suspicious characters?" Julian asks, his voice full of choked-back laughter. "Who are they? Just so I can tell my security who to watch out for."

I elbow him hard. This situation doesn't need him adding fuel to the fire. Besides, I'm more interested in how he used the words "illicit incursion" with a straight face.

Steffen eyes Julian up and down, and I just know he's going to say something amazing. Something I can hold over my stepfather's head from now until the day I die. I look around for Mom. She should really be here for this.

"Let's not get into that," Percy interjects calmly. "Steffen, can we safely assume you didn't notice Dustin, er, flirting with Rob?"

"Chasing him around the house, more like," Brandt says. "Flinging himself into his path."

Steffen's gaze comes back to me. "Are you Rob?"

I offer my hand. "Robert Sarris."

Not only does he not shake my hand, he also hesitates to introduce himself.

"Steffen," Brandt says, and Steffen heaves a put-upon sigh and shakes my hand.

"Steffen Smith," he introduces, and Percy laughs.

"At least you didn't say John Smith. It's okay, Stef. These people are trustworthy."

Steffen eyes me and Julian again, then nods. "Steffen Draco."

Wow. Apparently he really does think we're going to try to steal his identity. I wonder if he's been screwed over before or if he's just paranoid.

"Great to meet you."

"So Dustin gave up on the security guard and decided on you, did he?"

What? My gaze shoots to Dustin. What security guard? And why does Steffen have so many stories of Dustin and other men?

"Steffen," Dustin says sweetly, although I do believe his eyes are actually emitting laser beams. "Did you know that Rob is an English professor?"

"That's nice," Steffen replies, clearly not that interested. "You'll have things to talk about. Do you teach here in the city?" His gaze goes over my shoulder.

I don't get a chance to reply. Dustin's on a mission. "He teaches at the same college I go to. In fact, I've been in several of his classes."

That gets Steffen's attention, and relief crosses his face. "So you knew each other before tonight? That's great. You're not really a stranger, then. Phew! I guess it wasn't *that* stupid for Dustin to give you his phone." He frowns. "Wait… you're an English professor?"

I nod. I can see where this is going. Dustin has clearly spoken to his family and friends about his crush on me. Is it wrong that I find that endearing and flattering?

His gaze moves to Dustin, and he leans in to whisper loudly, "Is he *your* English professor?"

Dustin whispers back, "Yes. And you don't need to whisper. But you do need to shut up."

When Steffen turns back to me, he's grinning widely. "It's very nice to meet you. I have to say, I think Fabian is right, but you're still a good-looking man."

I'm beginning to think that talking to Steffen is just an exercise in patience. Who's Fabian, and what was he right about?

"Uh… thank you?"

"You're welcome." He glances from me to Dustin and back again. "Does this mean you're dating now?"

"Yes."

"No."

Dustin and I answer at the same time, then glare at each other.

"We're not dating," I insist. "We're just going to get to know each other better. As friends."

"We're dating," Dustin tells Steffen. "He's just being stubborn and making up all these stupid rules. Sorry, 'conditions.'" He pulls a face as he makes air quotes.

"Rules?" Steffen goes back to being suspicious. "What kind of rules? Is this some BDSM thing? Rules are good in BDSM. You need to discuss your limits beforehand and lay out the things you're not willing to do. Make sure you pick a safe word, and don't be afraid to use it. And if he ignores your safe word, shift and burn the place down to get away. You can call me, and I'll cover for you."

Julian starts to laugh. In fact, he's laughing so hard that tears are streaming down his face.

"BDSM?" Brandt asks. "That's the bondage stuff that was in the book you read to me, right?"

Julian chokes on his laughter, and all gazes turn to Percy. Quiet, demure, unassuming Percy. Who's seemingly into BDSM books.

He gazes back just as calmly as always, although his cheeks are a bit pink. "I read extensively," he says. "I'm not ashamed of that."

"Perhaps we can discuss recommendations," I reply, and all those gazes swing right back to me. I shrug. "What? I'm an English teacher. It would be remiss of me not to read widely."

Brandt's scowling now. "Listen, I don't usually interfere with Dustin's sex life, but—"

"Don't finish that sentence," Percy chides.

"But—"

"Percy's right, Grandfather. Seriously. Don't finish it."

Brandt rolls his eyes and heaves a huge sigh. These dragons sure do love being dramatic. "Fine. But promise me you'll be careful."

"I feel like now would be a good time for me to tell you that I'm not actually into BDSM," I suggest. "Well, maybe a little light spanking." I have no idea why I said that. This evening is spiraling completely out of control.

Dustin's expression brightens.

"Not that we'll be having sex," I add. "But you don't have to worry, regardless."

Smiling coyly, Dustin sidles up to my side and lays

that naughty hand back on my chest. "Spanking, huh? I like the occasional spanking." He rises on tiptoe and whispers, "Does this mean I should call you 'sir'?"

"Rules!" I yelp. "There are rules!" I can't remember what they are, since there's currently no blood in my brain, but I know I made a rule that would be helpful right this second.

"I thought they were conditions," Dustin purrs. The cheeky brat knows exactly what he's doing to me.

"Yes. Conditions. You… you… can't touch me! Inappropriate touching!"

He pouts and steps back, his hand falling away from my chest. I instantly miss it.

"You're not allowed to touch him?" Steffen asks, frowning. "I think you might be wrong about the whole dating thing."

"It's fine," Dustin assures him. "I just need some time. And his phone number." He turns back to me and extends his hand with his phone in it.

Unable to help myself, I glance at Steffen. "Is it okay?"

He smiles approvingly. "I like a cautious man. Go ahead."

I quickly input my number in Dustin's phone and send myself a text. "There. Now you have my phone number. Please make sure not to send me anything inappropriate." Visions of dick pics are dancing in my mind, and I can't decide if I want that or not. On the one hand, they would make it very hard to resist him. On the other hand… dick pic from a sexy, cute, funny, intelligent man who wants me. Either way, I'd be screwed.

"You're way too attached to that word," Dustin says, shaking his head as he reclaims his phone.

"What word?" I frown, trying to remember exactly what I said. I'm distracted by thoughts of his dick now.

"Inappropriate." He bats his eyelashes at me again, and I feel all resistance melting away. How does he do that? "It's only inappropriate if you make it that way."

Er… no. "That's not how it works."

He smiles. "Of course it is. I know these things; I've been around a long time." He pats my arm reassuringly. "Don't worry, you'll learn as you get older."

That sound you probably just heard was my brain exploding.

Fortunately, Percy sweeps in to rescue me. "So we're all set for lunch tomorrow, then? Dustin, send Rob a maps link to the estate so he can find it. Or," he glances at me, "we can send a car for you, if you prefer?"

"Thank you, but no. I like to get out for a drive occasionally, and it's been a while." Plus, if I have my own car, there's less chance Dustin can find a way to trap me at the estate. Not that I think he would, but… well, I don't think he *wouldn't*, either.

Sure enough, he's pouting. "This is ridiculous. We're all going to be traveling to the same place. Why doesn't Rob just come with us?"

"That would be interesting," Brandt says, and something about the gleam in his eye tells me it would be interesting for him, but something else entirely for me.

"I'd need my car to get home after," I prevaricate, but Dustin's got a particularly stubborn look on his face and shakes his head.

"I'd take you home after," he promises.

I snort. "Uh, no. I'm not committing to extended time alone with you and giving you my address until I know you've agreed to all my conditions." Which I need to finish thinking up before lunch tomorrow.

"Also," Percy says mildly, "you should ask Rob how he feels about flying on the back of a dragon before you try to get him to agree to it."

My jaw drops.

"It's not like he wouldn't have found out before he got on," Dustin protests. "He would have had a chance to change his mind at the last minute." He pauses. "Even if that would have been very rude and he probably would have agreed just to avoid offending Grandfather."

Admiration wells up in me… along with both relief and disappointment that none of that happened. Flying on the back of a dragon would be an indescribably amazing experience, but I think I'd need some time to build my courage first. And ask a lot of questions about the mechanics of it all.

But that doesn't mean I don't admire Dustin's ingenuity and sneakiness.

"Maybe we can do all that another time," I suggest. "Tomorrow, I'll just meet you at the estate."

Those lovely hazel eyes light up with pleasure, the otherworldly gleam in them so much more apparent now that I know he's a dragon. I actually feel stupid for not realizing earlier—I'd never met a dragon before, but I'd been told there's something different about their eyes.

"You're making plans for another time," he says happily. "Okay. Just so you know, I would be extremely careful while carrying you. No acrobatics or anything."

My stomach lurches at the thought. I've never been

a roller coaster kind of guy. But he's so earnest about it that I smile and say, "Great."

"Would you like to come with me to speak with Lihua Jiǎng?" He gestures toward a succubus across the room whom I've met a few times before. She's the matriarch of an influential family and generally quite acerbic, but Mom told me she's very generous with charity… she just likes to complain and intimidate while she does it. A conversation with her is still not a pleasant experience, and I can't imagine why Dustin would want to subject himself to that.

"Uh… why?"

He rolls his eyes. "Because she said earlier that she's interested in interspecies youth programs, and I think I can convince her to sponsor one near campus."

Julian perks up. "Really? She's already committed to a substantial donation for the city programs. I'd love to get one set up out that way—it's much easier for small-town kids to access—but given the expected participation numbers, I can't justify allocating the funding."

"What makes you think she'd be willing to sponsor a whole program?" I ask Dustin. Being a college town, there's a decent array of youth services in the area, but of course they're all aimed at human kids. Mom and Julian have told me in the past that even though community kids still sign up, they can never completely relax, and some of them who are still experiencing teen issues like spontaneous shifting can't sign up at all. A program that allows only community members would be much better for them.

"Because she grew up in the country and knows what it's like to not be able to access services," Dustin says blithely.

Julian's expression morphs to doubt as he glances across the room. "When she was growing up, I don't think services existed," he says. "It was more like 'grab your sword while you forage.'"

Percy makes a face. "I'm inclined to agree. She's considerably older than I am, and when I was growing up, youth programs just did not exist. You worked, you studied, or you helped your parents with the younger children. Sometimes all three."

Julian nods in agreement.

Dustin sniffs. "Trust me."

I *really* don't want to be part of a conversation with Ms. Jiǎng, but I also don't want Dustin to have to face her alone… and since he's compromised quite a bit tonight, I feel like I should step up too.

This would be a good way to start getting to know him, right? Contributing to a group discussion he's part of?

"I trust you," I say. "Let's go."

He looks at me with stars in his eyes, and I feel a thousand feet tall.

"She's not dangerous, is she?" Steffen asks out of the blue, his eyes focused with laser intensity on her. "I noticed a few people giving her a wide berth, but I thought that was just because of her sour face."

Percy closes his eyes and sighs.

"What?" Steffen asks defensively. "She can't hear me."

"Are you sure?"

Steffen stares a bit more. "Yes. If she could hear me, we'd know. She'd be pointing that sour face at us."

"That *is* why people avoid her, by the way," I tell

him. "And also because she has a sharp tongue to match."

"But she's a generous woman who's done a lot for the world," Julian reminds me. "A little respect wouldn't go astray."

Chastened, I nod. "Of course. You're right."

"Come on, then," Dustin says, not at all deterred by the interruptions. He starts across the room, and I follow, trying not to seem resigned and unwilling. At least I have a lovely view from here—I haven't had much opportunity to admire Dustin's backside, what with running away from him all night, but he does have a nice one.

That could be alllllll yours.

Damn voice of temptation. Two more years. I can hold out two measly years. Right?

CHAPTER SIX

Dustin

Lihua Jiǎng might well be a grumpy old woman, but as Julian says, she's a generous donor. I didn't get much chance to speak with her earlier, because I had one eye on the door, waiting for Rob to come back from wherever he was hiding, but she specifically indicated that she was interested in youth programs and also mentioned—entirely separately—that she'd been raised in the country. When Julian and I were speaking at the office the other day, the lack of funding available for programs outside cities concerned us both. This is the perfect time for me to begin my plans for the future *and* show everyone, once more, that I'm a reliable and responsible person.

If I succeed, this will be a real feather in my cap. And if I fail? Well, nobody thought it was possible anyway.

"Good evening again," I say cheerfully as I stop beside Ms. Jiǎng. Rob joins me, and I gesture to him. "I believe you know Rob?"

She eyes him. "We've met. It's been a while since the last time, since he goes out of his way to dodge me."

"I would never—" Rob splutters, but she's already turned away from him to look me up and down.

"Got what you wanted, did you?"

I smile sweetly. "That depends on what you think I wanted."

It's possible her lips curved up slightly, but it might have just been the light. "Him." She jabs a thumb in Rob's direction.

"Not entirely what I wanted, but it's a start. I need to wear down his complicated moral stance."

She snorts. "If anyone could do it, I'm sure it would be you."

"Thank you. That's very kind of you." I studiously ignore the strangled noise Rob makes. He's so cute. "We actually wanted to talk to you about the situation in Beresford."

"Oh?" She raises a brow. "What situation?"

"I'm sure you know Rob lives and works there, and as a student, I've had the opportunity to spend quite a lot of time both on campus and in the town. I noticed that it's a social hub for all the smaller towns and outlying farms."

"How very observant of you."

I bite the inside of my cheek to keep from laughing. I really like her. "Thank you. The point I'm getting at is that we believe—and Julian agrees—it would be the perfect location for a youth outreach program."

Her face doesn't change, but suddenly I can feel the full weight of her attention.

"Oh?"

"Yes. Rural youth is at higher risk for—"

"Yes, yes, I know the risks. What makes you think the town could support this program?"

Got her. I launch into a rundown of the rough figures I put together after Julian invited me to this party. I can sense Rob stiffening beside me, but I don't have time to work out what the problem is. All my attention needs to be on this right now.

"You've clearly done your homework," she says when my pitch winds down.

I look her dead in the eye. "This is important. The very least I can do is know what I'm talking about."

This time, there's no doubting that her lips turn up. It's barely a smile, but it's there, and there's approval in her gaze. "I suppose you want money from me."

"Your time would be of equal value. I estimate it will require about three hundred man-hours to get the program set up, and then between eighty and a hundred and fifty man-hours a week to run. How many hours can you give me?"

She snorts again. "I like you. Send me a full proposal with the numbers, and if my accountant approves, I'll fund your program."

Resisting the urge to leap in the air, pumping my fist, I incline my head to her. "That's very kind of you. You're not going to regret this."

Her considering gaze sweeps over me again, flicks to Rob, then settles on my face. "I don't think I will. Now be a good lad and fetch me a drink while I catch up with Erika's boy."

Pretending not to notice the way Rob grabs for my arm, I leave him to her tender mercies and go to the bar. I'm glad she sent me away; it gives me a chance to let my ear-to-ear grin free. This may just be the best night of my life.

"Hi." I smile at the bartender, who immediately smiles back. "I've been asked to get a drink for that woman over there." I half turn and gesture toward Ms. Jiǎng and Rob. "Do you happen to know what she's been drinking, or should we guess?"

His smile turns into a chuckle. "I know what she's drinking. You're not the first lackey she's sent over to me tonight." He turns away to begin preparing her drink, and Julian sidles up beside me.

"I saw you smiling," he says, gaze scanning my face. "That's good, right? Is it good?"

"Very good," I confirm. "She's provisionally agreed. I need to send her a full proposal."

Erika appears at his side in time to hear me, and she makes a sound I can only assume is a choked-off squeal.

"You wonderful, wonderful, genius man!" she exclaims, hugging me hard and planting a firm kiss on my cheek. I release the spell—along with a tiny distortion shield—and the kiss flutters to rest on my shoulder, the bold pink of gratitude and respect, unseen by anyone except me.

"Thank you," I say modestly. "It's not a done deal yet." But it will be. I can't let this opportunity get away.

"Do you have a proposal?" Julian asks anxiously as the bartender returns with Ms. Jiǎng's drink. I thank him, then turn back to Julian.

"Most of one. There are a few things I want to check, and then it needs to be gone over thoroughly. If I send it to you on Monday morning, could you review it before we send it to her?" I'm not an idiot—Julian does this all the time. His opinion is valuable.

He nods immediately. "Of course. Will that give you enough time? I know you have lunch tomorrow."

My grin is automatic. That's right, lunch with Rob. And my family and housemates, but hey, you can't have everything. "I'll have time," I tell him confidently. I might not sleep much, but I will definitely make time for the two most important things in my life right now: these programs and Rob.

"Lunch tomorrow?" Erika asks.

"I'll let you fill her in while I go rescue Rob." I lift Ms. Jiǎng's drink and then head back across the room. I'm halfway there when I hear Erika squeal—nothing stifled about it this time. I guess she's happy that Rob's giving me a chance to convince him a relationship between us would work.

Speaking of Rob, he greets me with far more enthusiasm than is warranted after a five-minute separation. I hand over the drink, then say, "What have you been chatting about?"

"You," Lihua Jiǎng says.

"Lihua has been trying to convince me to abandon my 'complicated moral stance,'" Rob adds.

"How nice. Did she succeed?"

"No." He crosses his arms across his chest, looking distinctly grumpy. It's so cute.

"We'll just have to keep working on it, then."

SOMETIME AFTER MIDNIGHT, Percy comes to find me, and I tear myself away from Rob—after making him promise he'll definitely show up for lunch tomorrow— and leave the party. We go back to the condos Grandfather uses here in the city, but while the others go to bed, I stay up a few more hours. I'm too wound up to sleep, and my proposal for the youth outreach program needs to be finished. I may as well put all this excess energy to good use.

In the wee hours, I finally crawl into bed and close my eyes, only to smile as images of Rob rise behind my closed lids. I can't believe how lucky I am. Only twelve hours ago, I was so sure I'd go my whole life without even having a meaningful conversation with him, and now not only did I spend most of the evening with him, I also kissed him… and we're planning for a future.

Sure, right now they're different futures, but I'm sure we'll end up on the same page once we're done negotiating. My page. With lots of snuggling and kissing and hot, dirty sex.

The two kisses he gave me are tucked safely in my wallet until I can bring them back to my hoard tomorrow. The one Erika gave me is there too, and I value it just as much—just in a different way. Where Rob's kisses are the beginning of what I hope will be a long and passionate romance, Erika's is an acknowledgment of my achievement. I did something they didn't even try, they were so convinced it wouldn't work.

I drift off to sleep with Rob's face smiling at me and the phantom touch of his kisses on my mouth.

WE LAND at the bottom of the garden at Here Be Dragons midmorning the next day. Despite going to sleep only an hour before dawn, I wasn't at all tempted to sleep in. Instead, I nagged Grandfather and Percy until they gave in, and we left the city an hour and a half before they'd intended.

Of course, I could have flown back by myself, but isn't the whole point of having family that they're supposed to be supportive when you need them? I need them now. My high from last night is wearing off, and doubts are creeping in. What if I can't convince Rob to give us a shot? He seemed very determined—after all, he managed to resist *me*, even though it was clear he was tempted. And his insistence on two years confuses me— does he really need that symmetry? I crushed on him for two years, so now he needs to resist me for another two? It makes no sense. And the part that keeps drumming through my brain is that even though he seems to want me, he doesn't want to want me. Why else would he be so resistant?

So I'm somewhat nervous as we shift back to biped form and walk up to the house. Percy slings an arm around my shoulders.

"You're quiet this morning."

Grandfather snorts. "I don't know how you can say that, when he was whining at us nonstop before." He ruffles my hair, and I make a mental note to tidy it properly before Rob gets here. I need to choose an outfit too—something that shows him I'm a responsible adult taking this whole situation seriously, but also that I'm sexy and fun. The whole spectrum of my person- ality needs to be represented by the clothes I wear to lunch.

"But he hasn't said much since then. Are you okay, Dustin?" Percy peers over at me. "Is something worrying you?"

I shake my head and force a smile. "I'm okay. Just

thinking of ways to convince Rob we're meant to be together."

Grandfather chuckles, and Percy's concerned expression relaxes. "You've made giant strides already," he points out. "Until last night, you couldn't even talk to him. Now he's coming here specifically to discuss the boundaries of your relationship."

"I still don't understand," Steffen breaks in. "Why does the relationship need boundaries?"

"Because Rob wants them," I say glumly.

"Baby steps," Percy insists. "Give him time to get used to the idea of being with you." He kisses the side of my head. "I'm going to go warn Kethe we've got an extra person for lunch."

As he quickens his stride, Stef keeping pace, Grandfather falls into step with me.

"You had a big night last night," he comments.

That's the truth. "Yep. Lots going on." I try not to hold my breath while I wait for his response. I'd really like to know that he sees what I'm achieving.

"Julian and Erika were very impressed with you."

"Were you?" I regret the words the second they leave my mouth.

"I'm *always* impressed with you, Dustin." The knot in my stomach relaxes slightly. "Even when you were doing things that made me want to lock you up, I was impressed by your ingenuity and creativity." He pauses. "But please don't go back to doing those things again. I'd much rather continue being impressed by your thoughtfulness and dedication to your people."

Well, that's a start.

We reach the patio, and before I can reply, there's a

shout from inside the house and then Kethe bursts out through the french doors.

"Is it true? You used your wiles on your professor?"

I squint and purse my lips. "I'm not sure. What are wiles?" My English is almost native-level good after all these years, but at moments like this I wish I was still using the translator spell.

Kethe waves impatiently. "I read about them in a book. They're like sexy tricks."

"Actually," Percy says from behind her, "they don't have to be sexy. To wile is to use cunning or trickery… but romance authors do tend to make more use of them than not, and so they have a reputation for being seductive."

We all look at him.

"Sorry. Didn't mean to steal focus."

Kethe turns back to me. "How can this be? Just last week, Fabian was telling us you couldn't even look at your professor without blushing. And now you've seduced him here for lunch?"

"Sadly, there was no seduction."

This time, all eyes turn to me. And they're all disbelieving.

"It's true," I insist. "Well, there was one kiss." I'm not counting the peck on the cheek, even if I do plan to hoard it. "But he was still determined afterward to have nothing to do with me, so I don't think it counts as seduction."

"So why is he coming, then?"

"Percy didn't tell you?"

She flushes. "I got so excited when I heard, I didn't wait for him to finish." She looks over her shoulder at him. "I'm sorry, Percy."

"Not to worry. We're all very invested in this, I think."

Aw, my family loves me.

"After two years of dramatic moping, we certainly are," Kethe affirms. I try not to be offended by that. Me, mope? Never. Sometimes my melancholy just overcomes me. "So why's he coming, then, if you haven't seduced him?"

"We're going to negotiate the terms of our relationship." I look around. "Could we go inside? I'd really like a cup of tea. And maybe some cake." Ever since Percy came to live with us and we had the Tea Trials, I've found that nothing's quite so nice as a hot cup of tea for a midmorning break. I still prefer coffee when I'm waking up, though.

Kethe, who manages the estate and looks after us all, makes an impatient noise and waves us inside. I can tell she'd really rather insist I tell her everything right this second, but she can't resist the urge to fuss over us. It's just part of who she is. If you infuriated her so much that she was coming after you with a deadly weapon, you could probably stop her in her tracks by asking for a hot drink and a snack. Not that I'm stupid enough to try to prove that theory. Kethe's even older than Grandfather, and she knows things.

Once I'm settled at the kitchen table with a mug of tea and a big slice of date loaf, I tell her everything. Percy and Grandfather have excused themselves, but Steffen joins me, chiming in unhelpfully every now and then. We're almost finished when I hear the sound of running footsteps, and a moment later Sophie skids into the kitchen, followed closely by Wil.

"You kissed your professor!" she squeals, throwing

herself at me for a big hug. I barely manage to move my mug in time. "It's like a fairy tale!"

We've spent a lot of time learning about Earth's pop culture in the past five years, but I can't seem to remember a fairy tale quite like this.

Wil must agree, because he asks, "Which fairy tale?" as he leans against the counter with a chunk of stolen date loaf in his hand.

"Pffft. Don't get caught up on technicalities," Sophie says. "The important thing is, you've *finally* made a connection with him."

"And he's coming for lunch," Steffen adds helpfully.

"Really?" Wil straightens. "You're okay with letting a strange human you've only met once come to the estate?"

Kethe throws a dishcloth at his head. It gets caught on one ear, and he grumbles as he unhooks it. "What? It's a valid question."

"Brandt and Percy both approved him, so I don't get any say," Stef replies, making me swing toward him in shock.

"I thought you liked Rob!" Does he really want to bar him from the estate? They seemed to get along so well last night.

Stef shrugs. "Liking someone is not a good reason to give them security clearance. The whole concept of betrayal exists because people do foolish things like that."

There's a little silence while we all try to gather the courage to ask. Unsurprisingly, it's Sophie who actually does it.

"Are you saying you don't like us? Or that you've

only given us security clearance because Brandt made you?"

Stef puts his mug to his mouth and tips it all the way up, draining the last of his tea, then says, "You don't have the necessary security clearance for me to tell you that."

Sophie's shriek echoes around the room. The intercom system buzzes, and Kethe goes to press the button. "It's okay. Steffen just upset Sophie."

"Do you need me to break them apart?" Grandfather's disembodied voice asks, and Kethe glances over to where Sophie is still sitting beside me, literally shaking.

"No, I think she's still paralyzed with rage. I can handle this."

Grandfather murmurs assent, and then Kethe bustles to get Sophie a mug of her favorite tea. She sets that down first, then goes rummaging in the back of a cupboard before triumphantly appearing with two packets of cookies.

I gasp. She's bringing out the store-bought imported cookies. The ones we're not allowed to eat because it hurts Kethe's feelings when we choose them over the ones she makes. The ones she keeps for special occasions and emergencies.

Sophie's gaze fixes on the cookies, and her tremors begin to lessen. I slide a glance toward Steffen, who's still sitting at the table like a big dumb rock. If Sophie was this mad at me and I'd been given a chance to escape, I would be gone. Instead, he grins at the cookies and says, "Could I have the Jaffa Cakes?"

The growl that comes from Sophie makes the furniture tremble, and Stef finally seems to wake up to exactly how much danger he's in.

"I mean… uh… Sophie should get them all. The Jaffa Cakes and the Tim Tams. All of them for her. Even though I missed out last time."

Wil gazes at Sophie for a moment, then says, "She can have my share too. I am totally on Sophie's side." He glances at Steffen. "Because you are an ass."

Kethe rolls her eyes. "Neither of you were going to get any to begin with. These are for Sophie so she doesn't go on a murder rampage. Soph, which ones do you want?"

I feel like that might be a trick question. Also, I'm super bummed that I don't get any. They're caramel Tim Tams, too, and those are my favorite. I need to order myself a stash from Amazon—they're worth the cost. The only problem is finding somewhere to hide them. I don't have Kethe's experience with that kind of thing, and in this house, there are no boundaries that won't be violated for chocolate cookies.

"Both," Sophie says, a hint of a snarl in her voice, and Kethe raises both eyebrows.

"Don't take that tone with me. You can't have both —Steffen's life isn't worth that much to me right now."

"What? Why?" Stef whines.

Kethe ignores him, but I lean over and whisper, "You don't like us and didn't want to give us security clearance."

"It's not exactly like that," he protests, then realizes he's just digging himself into a hole and shuts up, pouting.

Sophie picks the Jaffa Cakes—I think mostly to spite Stef, since she usually prefers Tim Tams—and it only takes a few bites and a big gulp of tea before the murdery vibe begins to fade. Kethe mutters about needing a new hiding spot while Wil and I stare longingly at the cookies, then gives in and passes around the rest of the Jaffa Cakes. Steffen keeps his mouth shut and stares at the tabletop.

"Where's Fabian?" I ask through a mouthful of deliciousness. "Normally he appears the second he smells chocolate."

"Not back yet from his hookup last night." Kethe shakes her head. "If he comes back with his clothes in the same condition as they were last week…" She lets the threat trail off, and I hope for Fabian's sake that his clothes are in good order.

"Okay," Sophie says at last, licking chocolate off her thumb. "I'm willing to let Steffen live a while longer, even if he is the biggest douchenugget alive. Let's go back to hearing about Dustin's professor."

I can't stop myself from grinning.

"So he's really coming here?" Wil asks. "He must like you a lot."

The grin fades.

"Weren't you paying attention?" Kethe demands. "He's coming because he thinks he and Dustin should just be friends. They're going to negotiate the terms of their relationship."

He scrunches up his face. "I don't think it works that way."

"It doesn't," Sophie agrees. "Why didn't you just seduce him? You're adorable. Nobody can resist you."

"He can," I say glumly, staring into the dregs of my tea. Kethe whisks the mug out of my hand and replaces it with a fresh one, full of steaming goodness, and I smile gratefully at her. Percy likes to say that there's not much that can't be solved with a good cup of tea, and honestly, he's right. "He resisted me even after we kissed."

"But he's willing to come to discuss the possibility of a relationship," Kethe says soothingly. "And it sounds to me like he's just having difficulty getting past you being a student. Give him time to process."

I sniff and have some more tea.

"In the meantime, we'll wow him," Wil encourages. "We'll tell him all about you and convince him you're… well, maybe we won't tell him *all* about you. We'll tell him the good things."

"Good things," I echo, remembering so many, many things I've done in the past that do not fit my new responsible persona. Rob cannot learn of them. He's already having trouble seeing me as an adult. "Um, remember that sometimes other species don't have the same definition of 'good' as we do."

"What does he like to eat?" Kethe asks. "I can make changes to the lunch menu."

I blink. "I… don't know. Does it matter?"

She scoffs. "I'm sure he'd be in a better mood if he was eating his favorite food. How are you going to seduce him if he's in a bad mood?"

Panic starts to creep in. "Why would he be in a bad mood? Are you saying my company puts him in a bad mood?"

"No, I'm saying we can put him in a *better* mood by feeding him food he likes. So what does he like?"

They all stare at me expectantly.

"Uh… he always gets pasta in the cafeteria at school." Although that might be because the pasta is one of the safer foods to eat there. "And last night, he seemed to like the shrimp canapés."

"Seafood pasta?" Sophie suggests, but Kethe shakes her head.

"I don't have any seafood on hand. We used it last week."

"Oh *no*," I gasp. "He's going to hate me. He's going to have a miserable lunch and never want to see me again!" I look wildly around the kitchen. "We need shrimp! Where can we get shrimp?"

"Uh-oh," Sophie says, and Wil puts down his mug and comes over to the table.

"Dustin, he's not going to hate you," he says patiently.

"And there's no such thing as a miserable lunch when I'm cooking," Kethe adds, her tone hard. "I'm going to give you a pass this time because this man makes your brain a noodle, but don't ever suggest that again."

"What will we feed him?" I plead. I am so close to convincing Rob we can be together. This lunch needs to be perfect.

"Leave it to me," Kethe insists. "Go upstairs and get ready. You want to be looking your best, right?"

I remember that Grandfather ruffled my hair earlier and decide she's right. There's not much I can do here in the kitchen—my cooking skills are average, at best—but I can trick myself out and show him exactly what he's missing.

"Good plan," I agree, abandoning my seat at the table. He's not going to know what hit him.

CHAPTER SEVEN

Rob

I'M NOT GOING to lie, I'm nervous as hell. That might seem dumb to you—it's just lunch with some very pleasant people whose company I enjoyed last night, right? But it's also lunch with a man who used to be my student and has made no secret of the fact that he wants a whole lot more from me. Plus there's that whole bit about me being the love of his life.

Personally, I think he's exaggerating. It doesn't take a lot of time spent in his company to know that Dustin is the dramatic sort—when he's not too tongue-tied to speak, that is. But that doesn't mean there isn't something between us, and I don't just mean the obvious sexual attraction. Dustin's right, we do need a chance to get to know each other... if only he wasn't a student still. I keep tripping on that bit.

The truth is, if he'd already graduated, or if he wasn't a student at all, I'd be all over him. Sure, at first I was concerned about the age gap, but now that I know I wouldn't be cradle snatching—the opposite, in fact—it doesn't worry me anymore. He's a very attractive man, intelligent, and based on what I saw last night, socially responsible. That would be enough to turn me on under any circumstances, but add the way he wants me, and I'm a goner. There's something about being desired, having someone go out of their way to make it clear that you're special, that really does it for me. I have mixed feelings about that—I know I shouldn't be thrilled to be chased, to basically be teasing Dustin. Sensible adults act on their attractions instead of playing foolish games that can only end in hurt feelings—or arrest for stalking. But I never intended to play games. If Dustin and I can't agree on terms today, I'll make it very clear that things can't proceed between us.

I don't think that will be a problem, though. I'm pretty determined to make this work, some way or another. Even if it means waiting two years to have sex.

Two. Whole. Years.

I push the thought—which makes me want to cry— aside and concentrate on my driving. According to the GPS, I'm getting close. Part of me is sorry I didn't take Dustin up on his offer to fly me here—because, hello, flying on the back of a dragon! Plus I wouldn't have had to drive for two and a half hours. Most of me, though, thinks driving was the right choice. Flying on the back of a dragon seems like something I might need to work up to, since I've never even gone zip-lining or anything like that. And it's good to have my own transportation with me, since this is a negotiation and Dustin already has enough power over me.

At least the drive home won't be as long. Beresford is a lot closer to where I am now than the city is.

"You have reached your destination," the GPS, which I've programmed to sound like an Australian man, announces, and I slow down and peer around. I've been driving along a stone wall for the last little while, and just up ahead, I can see a gate. Does that mean everything behind the wall belongs to the dragons?

Not a small country getaway, then.

I turn into the driveway and pull up in front of the gate. There's a post with an intercom system beside the driveway, so I reach out and hit the button. I really hope it's the doorbell and not a panic button or something.

Fortunately, barely three seconds pass before the speaker crackles to life with a woman's voice. "…doing it. Go away!"

"You go away! He's here to see Dustin, not you!"

"And I'm answering the door on Dustin's behalf."

"I'm in charge of security! I should be the one answering the door."

A scoff. "Oh, please. Dustin wants to impress this guy, not subject him to your crazy conspiracies."

I listen in fascination as the argument devolves into petty bickering about who's crazier. I think I recognize one of the voices as Steffen, the dragon from last night who thought I was going to rip off Dustin's identity.

Should I interrupt? I mean, eventually they'll realize I'm still here, right?

I clear my throat, hoping to get their attention discreetly.

It's a big fail.

As I listen to Steffen detailing all the ways the woman wins "nutjob of the year"—and honestly, if she's really done all the stuff he's saying, he might be right—I wonder if I'm going to have to call Dustin and let him know I'm here. Because it's been a few minutes now, and they don't seem to be tapering off.

"What are you two doing?" another female voice exclaims. "Didn't I hear the gate buzzer?"

The argument breaks off.

"Oh," Steffen says. "Yes, that's why we're here. We're just letting him in."

"Really? Because according to the control panel, the gate is still closed, and look, there he is on the camera, looking befuddled and likely terrified by you both."

Whoops—yep, there's the camera lens. I wave at it. "Hi." My voice comes out sounding somewhat uncertain, but thankfully not "befuddled and terrified." I can't wait to meet this woman, though. Anyone who can use "befuddled" in a sentence and make it seem normal has to be good fun.

"State your name and business," Steffen says officiously, and I can only blink in surprise.

"For fuck's sake, Stef, just let him in. You know who he is," the first woman says.

"There's a security protocol for a reason," Steffen insists. "It's there to protect us all."

"Yes," the second woman says, "but you can see who he is, and he's expected."

This seems like it could drag out for a while, so I say, "I don't mind. I'm, uh, Robert Sarris. Here for lunch? To visit Dustin." Maybe that can hurry things along.

"Satisfied?" the first woman asks, and a second later, the gates begin to swing open.

"You can park in front of the house," Steffen says. "I'll need to check your car before we let it near the others."

I'm still trying to work out what that's supposed to mean when the sound cuts off. Never mind. I'm sure I'll find out soon enough.

As soon as the gap is wide enough, I accelerate through. The driveway is ridiculously long, winding through the woods, and it's a few moments before I round a bend and the house comes into sight. If you can call it a house. "Mansion" is a much better fit. Or maybe "palace."

In other words, big.

Julian has serious money, so I've been in a lot of rich people's houses—I grew up in one. But this is next level. I guess it makes sense, since Brandt is the wing leader and basically runs his government from here.

I slow the car in front of the house and stop. There's not really anywhere to park; the driveway continues around the side of the building, where I'm guessing the entrance to a garage is, or at least a parking area. But Steffen said to park here, and upsetting a paranoid dragon doesn't seem like a wise thing to do, so I'm parking here. I turn off the engine and get out of the car, scanning the woods as I do. The trees provide a ton of privacy, which I imagine was a big selling point.

Slamming the car door, I turn to face the house… and force myself not to jump. Six wide stone steps lead up to a landing in front of massive double doors, and on that landing stand three people, attention fixed on me. One is Steffen, scowling so hard, I want to duck for cover behind my car. The other two are women, presumably the voices through the speaker, and they're both grinning widely.

What do I do now?

"Hello. I'm Rob," I say inanely. "Hi, Steffen. We met last night. Do you remember?" It's a stupid question, and normally I wouldn't ask it unless the person I was speaking to had suffered some kind of head injury right after we met, but given how antsy he seems to be, I figure it's better safe than sorry.

To my relief, his scowl lessens somewhat, and he stalks down the steps toward me. "I remember. I just need to check your car."

"Sure," I agree. "For what, exactly?" Explosive devices? Cameras? Rust?

"Don't worry about him," one of the women calls. "Just leave him to it. He can park it for you after, since he's going to be such a pain." They both come down the stairs as Steffen takes my keys. I move away from my car with a great deal of reluctance—here's hoping Steffen's inspection doesn't trash it.

The women descend on me with wide grins, and I seriously consider taking a step backward. They seem friendly enough, and definitely glad to see me, but that's weird, right? They don't know me.

"So you're Dustin's professor," the older one exclaims, hand outstretched. "I'm Kethe."

I shake her hand, relaxing slightly as I recall that Dustin has apparently spoken about me before. That's both embarrassing and flattering.

"Rob Sarris," I introduce myself, though she probably knows that.

"I'm Sophie," the other woman says, practically snatching my hand away from Kethe and pumping it eagerly. She's the first woman I heard over the speaker, the one who was arguing with Steffen. "We're so happy you're here. Hopefully this will get Dustin back to his usual self."

A pang of guilt strikes me. I know it's not my fault Dustin had a crush on me, but still, it's not great to hear that he hasn't been himself because of me—however indirectly.

"Don't be silly," Kethe says briskly. "His usual self flirted with everything that moved. Now that Rob's here, Dustin's only going to flirt with him."

"Oh, well, I don't know abou— Wait. Everything that moved? That's an exaggeration, right?"

"Not really," Steffen says as he comes up beside me. "Dustin's a flirty guy. Even with this weird no-fucking depression he's been going through, he still flirts. Not as much as before," he adds reflectively. "But just last night he flirted with the security guard."

A tiny swirl of jealousy knots in my gut. It's stupid and immature, but I can't help it. I want to be the only person Dustin flirts with. And if that's not a sign of me being fucked-up, I don't know what is. On the plus side, "no-fucking" surely means what it sounds like, right? I don't even feel guilty about this—refraining from sex never hurt anyone, and Dustin has a perfectly good right hand. The jealous, possessive part of me loves the idea that he met me and stopped fucking anyone else.

The sensible part of me is shaking his head in shame.

Resolving to be a better person, I say, "Dustin's behavior is his choice. I would never suggest he change anything about himself for me—or anyone else." It's pompous and condescending, but the intention is good.

Steffen snorts and goes back to whatever he's doing to my car. The women exchange glances.

"Weeeeeeeell," Kethe says. "I suppose. But I definitely like post-migration Dustin better than pre-migration Dustin."

"Mm, no." Sophie shakes her head. "I liked pre-migration Dustin just as much as post-migration Dustin. But I wouldn't have trusted him to look after a brick. Post-migration Dustin is much more responsible. But post-professor Dustin was too mopey for my liking. I'd really appreciate if you could do something about that."

I honestly don't know what to say.

"What are you *doing*?" Dustin shrieks from the open front door, and we all look up at him.

"Hi, Dustin!" Sophie waves. "We're just saying hello to Rob."

"Hi, Dustin," I say, also waving. Mostly because it seems like the thing to do.

He runs down the steps and skids to a stop beside us, glaring at Sophie and Kethe. "And you had to say hello outside? You couldn't invite him in and let me know he was here? What have you been saying?" He rounds on me. "What have they been saying? It's probably not true. I'm a delight!" He pouts, hands planted on his hips, and my heart melts even as my cock twitches. How can anybody possibly be this adorably sexy?

"You are," I soothe. "You're utterly delightful."

The pout turns to a smile, and he sidles over and wraps his arm around mine. "Aw, aren't you sweet?" he coos. "I'm so sorry they've kept you out here. Come inside and let me get you something to drink. How was the drive?" He tugs me toward the front steps, ignoring the way Sophie and Kethe grin and whisper to each other. Given the way shifter hearing works, he can prob-ably hear what they're saying anyway.

"Good. Uh, long, but there was no traffic or anything."

"That's great. Did nobody tell you where to park your car? Honestly, they're the worst. I'm so sorry."

"Uh, no, Steffen wanted to check the car first."

He stops dead just as we reach the steps and sighs. "I'm so sorry," he repeats. "Just give me a second. Feel free to go inside if you want." He untangles his arm from mine and stomps over to where Steffen is peering at the front side panel of the car, hand hovering over the surface, fingers stretched wide. I have no idea what he's doing, but I assume it involves a spell of some kind. From what I've learned in the past few years, dragon magic is very different from what I grew up seeing sorcerers do.

"Steffen!" Dustin hisses, loud enough for me to hear clearly. "Could you maybe not ruin this for me?"

Steffen straightens. "How am I ruining it? He's not upset. That's good—you don't want to get involved with someone who doesn't take security seriously."

"Please, please, just act normal for a few hours. There's no security risk. His car is fine."

Steffen nods. "I'm sure it is," he placates. "I'm nearly finished, and then I'll park it with the others. You head on inside and show him around. Keep him away from the security control room and the hoards—his security clearance doesn't cover those."

Dustin makes a sound that could indicate he's about to attack, then opens his mouth, closes it again, jabs a finger in Steffen's direction, and spins on his heel to stomp back over to me. He looks like an angry kitten, but I'm not dumb enough to underestimate him anymore. Adult dragons can do a lot more damage than angry kittens.

By the time he reaches me, his teeth and fists are no longer clenched, but there's still a flush of angry color on his cheeks. It's a lovely contrast to his golden hair and bright eyes.

"Sorry about that," he says. "Steffen will park your car. And it will be in perfect working condition when you leave, I swear. The spell he's using isn't destructive in any way."

"It's fine," I assure him. "You look good today." I say it mostly to distract him, but it's true—and the way he reacts makes me want to compliment him some more. His spine straightens, a smile blooms, and he makes an aborted primping gesture.

"Thank you. So do you. But then, you always look good. Come inside."

I obediently walk up the steps, aware of the women following us a few paces back. Dustin ushers me through the huge double doors and into an entrance hall that literally makes my jaw drop. It stretches up the height of the house, four floors, the exposed rafters high above stark in contrast to the massive chandelier suspended among them. There's a giant stone fireplace on one wall, and the floors above have open galleries over-looking a very comfortable-looking seating area. This one space is more than twice the size of my entire three-bedroom house.

"Wow."

"It's pretty great, isn't it? We looked at a lot of places. Some of them were closer to the city, which would have been good, since Grandfather has to be there for most of the week, but this is more private, has more space inside and out, and just feels right, so we picked it. And it doesn't take long to get to the city when you're flying." He pauses. "We have had some trouble with finding a good place to land and launch in the city, though. The first place we were using had to be abandoned after the whole naked dragon ride thing."

I really want to ask, but I'm also not sure I want to know. Especially if Dustin was involved.

"Rob!"

I turn in the direction of the voice, glad for the interruption. I'm pretty sure I would have asked, and I might have regretted it.

Percy strolls out of a hallway, smiling. As always when I'm in his company, a tiny bit of tension melts away. I used to think it was because he was the lucifer, but I guess it's just him. Some people are naturally soothing.

Dustin chooses that moment to lean against my side, and my entire body goes into overdrive. Soothing is definitely not the word I'd choose to describe him. Almost without thinking, I wrap an arm around his shoulders.

So much for the no-inappropriate-touching rule.

Condition. I mean condition, not rule.

Friends put their arms around each other, right? I'm sure they do. So technically, this isn't inappropriate.

Dustin's hand slides down and gropes my ass, and I sigh. There goes any hope of being appropriate.

Mustering every ounce of willpower I possess, I remove his hand from my posterior and step sideways, putting some distance between us.

"Hello, Percy. Thank you for inviting me today."

Percy shakes his head at Dustin, a long-suffering smile on his face, then turns his attention back to me. "You're most welcome. We had a lovely time last night —your parents throw wonderful parties."

"They do," I agree, although my enjoyment last night was tempered by the constant running and hiding.

"Excuse me, why didn't you thank me for inviting you?" Dustin demands. His hands are back on his hips.

"Because you didn't invite me. Percy did."

"That's true." Percy nods solemnly. "But let's not stand around debating it. Come out to the terrace, Rob. It's such a nice day, we thought we'd eat out there. Lunch isn't quite ready yet, so there's time for a drink." His gaze drifts over my shoulder. "Ah, there you are, Kethe. I wondered where you'd got to."

"I was supervising the children," she says cheerfully, coming to stand with us. "They would have left poor Rob at the gate all day."

"As opposed to standing in the driveway?" Dustin mutters.

Kethe raises her eyebrows. "What was that?"

"Nothing. Let's go out to the terrace." He grabs my hand and tugs. As I follow, I shoot a questioning glance at Kethe.

"I run the house," she tells me, and that's pretty much all I need to know. After Mom married Julian, we had a housekeeper, and I know better than to cross the person who prepares your meals and does your laundry.

We walk down a wide hallway lined with doors. I sneak a peek through a few of them and find comfortable, well-furnished receiving rooms—living spaces, a library, an office. The house is clearly set up to accommodate a lot of people, letting them congregate in both large and small groups.

"How many of you live here?" I ask.

"Full-time? Eight," Dustin says. "Me, Grandfather and Percy, Kethe, Steffen, Sophie, Wil, and Fabian. But because this is the main government seat, we have a lot of visitors. And of course anyone who needs a place to stay is welcome here. Right now, it's just us."

We enter a really lovely sunroom. The entire back wall is glass panes, with french doors opening out onto a paved terrace that leads down to a gorgeous garden and lawn. Beyond that are the woods. If I remember right from my glance at Google Maps, there's a national park back there somewhere too.

At one end of the sunroom is another fireplace, and I can just imagine how amazing this room would be to curl up in during a winter storm.

We go outside, where Brandt sits on an outdoor sofa, his feet on a coffee table and a glass of something in his hand as he chats to another man. They both glance over at us, and Brandt lifts his glass in salute.

"Welcome, Rob! Come and have some of this fancy water."

"It's very refreshing," Kethe says, leading the way. "Cucumber, blueberry, and mint. I mixed it up myself." She pours a glass from the giant pitcher on the table and hands it to me. Since everyone is staring, I guess I'm supposed to taste it immediately, so I sip.

"Oh, that's delicious," I say, surprised. I mean, it's water with cucumber and berries in it. I wasn't expecting anything special. But it really is refreshing.

"Sit," Kethe urges. "I'll go check on lunch." She disappears back into the sunroom, and the rest of us find seats around the coffee table. There are two of the squishy-looking couches and a few armchairs. Dustin herds me toward the other couch. I know what he's doing, but there's no way to avoid it without making a scene, so I sit on the couch and try to keep some distance between us when he plants himself beside me.

"Rob, this is Wil," Percy says, and I lean over to shake his hand. He looks normal, but in the fifteen or so minutes since my arrival, I've learned that when it comes to dragons, normal is relative.

"Hi," he says. "So you're Dustin's professor." His gaze skims me, and he purses his lips. "I think Fabian was right."

At the back of my mind, I vaguely remember Steffen saying something similar last night, and I'm on the verge of asking what Fabian was right about when Dustin snaps, "You and Fabian don't know what you're talking about."

Okay then. Leaving that topic alone.

"This is such an amazing space," I say instead, my gesture encompassing the terrace, the garden, and the woods. The paved area stretches half the width of the house and would be perfect for summer parties. There's a ten-seat table already set for lunch, and potted shrubbery and flowers spread around in what at first looks random but actually cleverly acts as area separators.

"We love it," Brandt says. "Especially when we have parties. And the lawn gives us plenty of space to launch and land."

"I've been told your dragon forms are impressive." I stare out at the huge lawn. I don't think they need a running start to launch like a plane does, so they must really be big to need this much space.

"Some are more impressive than others," Dustin says with that flirty note back in his voice. Sophie coughs.

"Thank you, Dustin; I've always considered myself to be impressive," she says, and he flips her off.

"Anytime you want, I can shift and show you my

dragon form," Dustin promises, shifting a little closer. I resist the urge to move away—there's only a few inches between me and the armrest, and I need those for when he's close enough to climb into my lap. It's not hard to resist, because I like being this close to him.

"That's very kind of you. I imagine if our friendship continues, I'll take you up on that."

"Friendship?" Wil asks. "Dustin wants a lot more than friendship from you, Professor."

"You can call me Rob," I tell him, wondering if I can avoid the rest of what he said. I'd really rather work out the details of our relationship in private, rather than with all Dustin's housemates—family?—listening and contributing.

"Don't worry," Dustin says confidently. "It's going to be more than friendship. Rob just needs to set his 'conditions.'" He makes air quotes, and I sense any control I might have had slipping rapidly away.

"Ohhhhh." Wil nods knowingly. "As long as none of those 'conditions'"—he also makes air quotes—"involve illegal or morally depraved activities. Dustin's not that kind of dragon." He pauses. "Anymore."

"Of course they won't involve illegal or morally…" I trail off as my brain catches up, then look at Dustin, who bats his eyelashes at me. "Anymore?"

He lays a hand on my thigh. "Don't listen to him. He's exaggerating. The laws at home were different, anyway." His hand inches higher, and my mind spins.

"Uhhh…"

"Lunch!" Kethe calls, saving me from having to either think or stop Dustin from feeling me up in front of his grandfather. "Could I have some help, please?"

I leap to my feet. "I'll help you!"

"No, you won't," Percy says firmly, rising with a lot more grace than I did. "You're our guest. Please make yourself comfortable at the table. Dustin and Wil will help Kethe."

Dustin makes a sound of protest, but Percy shoots him a stern look, and he closes his mouth on whatever argument he was about to make.

Relieved and grateful for the reprieve, I join Brandt, Percy, and Sophie at the table. I'm tempted to try and maneuver things so I'm sitting between two of them, but I doubt they'd allow it—and anyway, I'm here to get to know Dustin better. If that means I need to spend the meal peeling his hand off my leg, so be it.

Or you could just leave it there, the evil side of me whispers. *See how far he'll go. You know you want to. You'll enjoy it.*

I push the notion aside. Until I've outlined my boundaries and made it clear to Dustin that things can't get sexy between us until he's graduated, I need to be careful not to lead him on. My morals might be losing this battle, but I can't abandon them completely.

Kethe comes out a few minutes later, followed by Wil, Dustin, and Steffen, all bearing laden dishes that smell incredible. There's an interval of confusion as the food is passed around and served and everyone finds a seat, and then we dig in.

As I expected, Dustin is beside me, his chair scooched closer than necessary. On my other side is an empty seat, and I do a quick head count. Everyone I've met is here. I guess the only person missing is Fabian, who both Wil and Steffen think is right about something that I'm not privy to.

As though reading my mind, Wil asks, "Fabian not home yet?"

Kethe shakes her head. "No. Who knows where he is. I just hope he's not tied to a pipe in someone's basement again."

I freeze with my fork inches from my mouth. Again?

"That wasn't so bad," Brandt disagrees. "It was worse when his hookup left him naked in the woods and he had to walk into the nearest town with no clothes on to find a phone."

Oh. My. God.

"Or what about the time he went to that orgy and—"

"Hi, everyone! Oh great, I'm just in time for lunch."

My head whips around so fast, I swear I hear the vertebrae crack. An unassuming-looking yet somehow vaguely familiar brown-haired man saunters out onto the terrace. He looks like he's just rolled out of bed—hair mussed, beard growth, clothes wrinkled and slightly askew.

"Good afternoon, Fabian. We were just talking about you," Percy says dryly. "I'm glad to see you're unharmed and not in police custody."

Fabian nods. "Me too. Last night was pretty ordinary, so there was no danger of arrest. But I slept late this morning, and then we had another round before I left." He slides into the chair beside me, and I catch a distinct whiff of sex. This guy really must be completely comfortable with his sexuality, because if I can smell it, so can everyone else, and he doesn't seem to care.

Sure enough, there's a wave of wrinkling noses. "Couldn't you have showered before joining us?" Steffen asks pointedly.

Reaching for the nearest serving dish, Fabian shakes his head. "Nope. Then I would have missed lunch." He suddenly seems to notice me beside him, smiles, then does a double take. "Hey, I know you! You're Dustin's professor!"

"Yes. Rob Sarris." I think about offering to shake hands, but both of his are full right now.

"What are you doing here?" He leans forward to look past me at Dustin. "What is even happening?"

"Fabian…" Brandt sounds pained. "Could you at least pretend to be polite?"

"I'm very polite," Fabian declares indignantly. "I recognized him and everything." He finishes dishing food onto his place, puts down the serving dish, and offers me his hand. "I'm Fabian."

I really want to ask him if he's washed his hands since round two. Would that be rude? There's only so long I can hesit—

"Please tell me you at least washed your hands before coming to the table," Sophie demands. "Don't make me give you another lecture on hygiene."

Fabian rolls his eyes. "Of course I did. Anything is better than listening to you drone on about bacteria."

Grateful beyond words to Sophie, I shake his hand as he continues, "I still think it's stupid. It's not like we can catch anything."

"Human habits," Percy reminds him. "We're trying to fit in. And anyway, you might not be able to catch anything, but Rob here can. If you're going to interact with humans, you need to protect them."

"I did," Fabian protests. He turns back to me. "I did," he assures me, then studies me closely. "Is Dustin in some kind of trouble? Is that why you're here? But he's not in any of your classes this year. Are you fundraising for the university?" His eyes suddenly go wide. "Oh *fuck*. You know about us, right? I just assumed you wouldn't be here if you didn't already know… but then I said I couldn't catch bacteria… and Percy said humans…" He looks completely horrorstruck.

"It's fine, Fabian," Brandt says. "Rob knows. His stepfather is an incubus."

Fabian sags, hand to his chest. "Thank fuck."

I feel like I should pat him on the shoulder or something, but I don't want to. He really does smell quite strongly of sex, and after hearing about orgies and naked woods escapades and being tied to a pipe, I can't be sure his shirt wasn't part of whatever sexual antics he got up to this time.

He picks up his fork to start eating, and my gaze catches on the ring he's wearing. It's a simple silver band engraved with a word in flowing script. I frown. Does that say…?

"Are you wearing a purity ring?" The question bursts from me in disbelief, and the table falls silent. All eyes focus with laser-like intensity on Fabian's hand.

He glances at it and nods. "Yep."

"I… I don't know what to say," Kethe murmurs.

"How did you know it's a purity ring?" Dustin asks me.

"It says 'purity.'"

He leans over me and grabs Fabian's hand to study the ring. I narrowly avoid getting stabbed by Fabian's (thankfully now empty) fork.

"Huh. It does. How did I never notice that?" He lets go of Fabian but stays snuggled up close to my side. I'm too distracted to care, which is actually kind of a shame.

"I never noticed either," Wil says. "Anybody?"

There's a wave of shaking heads and murmured

dissents. Fabian's the only one still eating—everyone else seems too shocked. Which, given the little I've heard about his sexual escapades, is understandable.

"Fabian," Sophie begins, "*why* are you wearing a purity ring?"

"It won't come off."

Brandt groans and buries his face in his hands.

"Okay." Sophie pauses. "We'll come back to that in a minute. What I meant was, why did you put it on in the first place? You've never abstained from sex in all the time I've known you." She glances over at me. "And that's a long time."

Fabian shrugs. "It was a miscommunication. I was at the mall, and this guy had a stall in the middle of the concourse. He was passing out pamphlets and selling jewelry, and I stopped to look, because I had to leave so much of my hoard behind." Sadness crosses his face. "I thought maybe I could buy some new pieces."

Everyone nods sympathetically. Dustin leans up to whisper in my ear. "Fabian hoards rings."

I nod sympathetically too. Poor Fabian.

"So the man asked me if I'm pure of heart," Fabian continues, "and I said 'of course,' because I *am*. I've never deliberately hurt anyone, and I give time to helping people. Right?"

"Right," Brandt says, and Wil and Dustin nod. Steffen looks dubious, but that could just be his resting expression. The others just look impatient.

"Well, he got really excited when I said that and asked me a bunch of questions about whether I was committed to being pure and willing to wear a symbol of my purity for all to see. And I was on board with that, so I said 'sure' and bought this ring." He holds up his hand and tips it so the silver catches the sunlight. "It's pretty."

"Very pretty," Kethe agrees. "When did you realize he meant sexual purity?"

Fabian sighs. "Two days later. I went clubbing and the men were all over me." He turns to me and explains, "I don't usually have problems finding a hookup, but this was way out of the ordinary. I could barely turn around without someone rubbing up on me." He pauses expectantly, so I make a sound of what I hope is sympathetic agreement. Is this even real? Am I having some kind of hallucination? Did I hit my head and end up in a coma? Is my mother even now sobbing over my unresponsive body as Julian swears to find a way to wake me?

Dustin's hand slides up my thigh, and the speed with which all the blood rushes from my head answers my question. I doubt hallucinated arousal would be so intense.

"Anyway," Fabian continues, "I went home with someone and we fucked, and then after he was all douchey, crowing about how he was such a stud he'd conned me out of my celibacy." He snorts. "Celibacy! As if I could be celibate. It would be such a waste."

"Then what happened?" Dustin asks with far too much fascination. "Was he a good fuck at least?"

Fabian see-saws his hand. "Average. Which I told him when I asked what he was talking about. And then he asked me why I was wearing a purity ring if I wasn't celibate, and the truth came out." He looks at the ring again. "I was so disappointed."

"I'm sure you were," Kethe says with absolutely no sympathy whatsoever. "But Fabian, you've been wearing that ring for years."

He nods. "Yes. I bought it about a year after we moved to Earth."

"And you tried to take it off right after you found out it was supposed to be a symbol of celibacy?"

He nods again. "It's stuck. I guess I should have gone for the bigger size, but the guy who sold it to me said it didn't matter if it was a bit snug since I would be wearing it all the time anyway, and I wouldn't want to risk losing it because it was slightly loose." He picks up his fork again and resumes eating.

"Fabian," Sophie says slowly, "why haven't you tried to have the ring removed at any time in the past four years?"

He blinks at her. "I have. I try to take it off every few days. It's stuck."

"I wish you'd mentioned it to me sooner," Brandt says. "I could have helped. I'm sure we can find a way. What methods have you used? Some spells?"

The blank look on Fabian's face gives me a hint of what he's going to say. "I pull it. It doesn't come off. What do you mean, methods? Why would I use a spell to get a ring off?"

"To get it off," Percy explains patiently as everyone else groans. "Brandt and I will help you after lunch. I bet cold water and butter will do the trick, but if not, I'm sure Brandt has a spell that will."

Fabian seems surprised. "I never thought of trying something like that. When it wouldn't come off, I just figured it wasn't hurting anyone. I had better things to do with my time than worry about it."

Dustin squeezes my thigh. "Fabian is our record keeper," he explains. "He's in charge of documenting everything important and maintaining past records. And research."

My nerd brain comes to life. "That's fantastic," I say, turning to Fabian. "You must know so much. I'd love to learn more about dragon culture, but it's not like there's a course I can sign up for."

"I can teach you everything you need to know," Dustin protests.

"I could teach a course about dragon culture," Fabian says at the same time. "That would be fun." He looks over at Brandt. "Could I?"

"I don't see why not." Brandt turns to Percy. "Do you?"

"I like the idea," Percy says. "There would need to be some ground rules. Let's talk about it while we're trying to get your ring off."

"Great!" Fabian's all smiles, and I'm still trying to get my head around everything that's happened in the past fifteen minutes—not to mention eat my lunch—when he turns back to me again and says, "So tell me, why are you here?"

"Percy invited me. My parents hosted the fundraiser he and Brandt and Dustin—and Steffen—attended last night."

His eyes widen. "Wow. That's a coincidence! Did you know Dustin was a dragon before last night?" He leans around me again to talk to Dustin. "Did you know your professor was part of the community?"

"No to both questions," I say, forestalling Dustin. I need to regain control of this conversation somehow. "It was a surprise for both of us."

"Great surprise, though. Dustin's obviously gotten over his stupid brain mush and seduced you. Did you stay here last night? No, you said Percy invited you… Dustin, shame on you. You should have been the one to invite your hookup over for lunch."

"We haven't hooked up. We're not going to hook up." I make my voice as firm as I can, trying to be strong despite the temptation of Dustin's body pressed up against mine. I deliberately don't look at him, almost certain his adorable pout will have made a reappearance.

Fabian frowns and looks from me to Dustin and back. "But… why? Dustin's been gaga over you for years."

I sigh. Wil comes to my rescue. "I'll catch you up later. The short story is that Rob's come over so he and Dustin can, uh, discuss the direction their relationship is going to take."

Squinting, Fabian asks, "Is that a euphemism for sex? Is this the whole naked dragon ride thing again? Because that one was better. 'Discuss the direction of the relationship' is boring."

Percy whimpers. "Never. Not ever. I will never live that down." Brandt pats his hand.

I feel like I'm missing something.

"It's not a euphemism for sex," I insist. "No sex. There will be no sex."

"You're breaking my heart," Dustin whines.

"Why no sex?" Fabian asks, his face screwed up in confusion. "Sex is the best."

"This is the best day of my life," Sophie says. "The only way it could get better is if one of Stef's conspiracy theories comes true and someone fleeing from assassins leaps out of a helicopter or something and lands in the garden."

There's a brief pause as we all look up at the sky and then around the garden. Nobody appears, fleeing from assassins or otherwise.

"Well, that's disappointing." Sophie stands. "I'm going to start clearing up."

"We're not all finished," Steffen complains. I hastily scoop up more food.

"Are we actually eating, though?" she counters. "We're just letting the food get cold while we talk about Fabian's sex life and Dustin's lack thereof."

"Sophie's right," Kethe says, also standing. "Let's clear up now, and I'll make a hearty snack for later, after Dustin and Rob have had their talk and Fabian's got that ring off."

"Good idea!" Dustin leaps to his feet, knocking his chair over. I guess we're having our conversation now.

Well, fuck.

I'M SO NERVOUS. That's why I was quieter than usual during lunch. That's because this conversation has been looming large. How am I supposed to handle it? What if Rob's "conditions" are ridiculous? What if he's actually serious about us just being friends? I'm so close to happiness—I can't let it get away from me now.

I lead Rob to one of the informal sitting rooms and make sure to cast a killer privacy spell as I close the door. The last thing I need is anyone listening in on this. That's why I chose this room—there are others with better views from the windows, but this one only has a small window that overlooks the paved parking area. It's a lot less likely that anyone will be "casually" walking by and stop to gawk.

"So," I say, walking over to where he's sitting in one of a pair of armchairs. I sit in the other and wish he'd chosen the couch, where I could snuggle up to him. He's proven susceptible to my touch. With two feet of space between us, I'm not sure I'll be successful in convincing him to take a chance on me. "Tell me what 'conditions' you've come up with."

He studies me for a moment, his gaze thoughtful. "I really wish you'd stop using air quotes when you say conditions."

"I'm sorry. I'm just struggling to understand why you're so determined we not be together. If you don't want me, please say so." My heart clutches in my chest at the mere thought, but I force myself to continue. "Or is it something else? Are you aromantic? Or asexual, and I'm coming on too strong?" Because that's something I can work with. A relationship is only healthy if all parties are happy, which means open communication and discussion of what everyone needs.

Which is what he's been trying to do.

I'm such an asshole.

I put my hands in my lap and give him my full attention.

"It's nothing like that," he assures me. "My main concern is that you're a student at the college where I teach. I know you don't actually fit the profile of the students the rule was created to protect, but nobody else knows that. As far as they're concerned, you're a twenty-year-old and I'm more than twice your age and potentially in a position of authority over you."

I can't dispute that, but it seems a poor reason to give up any chance of being together. "What if I promise that on campus, I treat you as I would any other professor? It's not likely that we'll even have any reason to see each other, unless I run into you in a hallway or something."

"That's one of my conditions. No crossing boundaries on campus."

"Okay." I can do that. I'll just continue gazing longingly at him when I see him in the cafeteria. Nothing has to change.

"No inappropriate touching, as I've already said."

"On campus?" I'm confused. "I thought we agreed I wasn't even going to come near you on campus."

"Anywhere. Before we cross any sexual lines, we need to get to know each other properly. We're only going to have sex if this turns out to be an otherwise serious relationship."

"No." I'm surprised by how firm my voice is. It's his turn to look confused.

"What do you mean, no? You can't force me to have sex with you."

"Of course not." I shake my head. "But for me, sex is an important part of a relationship. Whatever that looks like—if it's anal penetration, or hand jobs and blowjobs, or even just me jacking off while you watch—it's something that needs to happen naturally. You can't dictate that it can only happen when a set of arbitrary targets are met. Especially when you haven't told me what those targets are and why you've set them."

Consternation crosses his face, followed by a wry smile. "Your logic and intelligence are so very attractive."

Joy bursts in my chest. People have desired me for my looks, my charm, my body, my connection to Grandfather, or any combination of those things… but never my intelligence. It just goes to show how right my instincts were to fixate on Rob.

"Thank you," I manage. "I… I guess this will be easier if we're both just honest about what we want. I think you're amazing and I want a relationship. Not a casual sexual fling and not a friendship. I understand that you don't know me well and probably want to spend time learning who I am, but isn't that part of dating?" There. My cards are all out on the table. I try not to hold my breath while I wait for his response.

He's quiet for a moment. "I know you think I'm foolish to be worried about the fact that you're a student," he begins. "Logically, I agree with you that it's not a real issue. But it's a hurdle I can't bring myself to overcome so easily. You're a student where I teach, and that's a line I've spent twenty years not crossing."

Like someone bashed the idea into my brain, I suddenly understand. "Is that the only thing holding you back? The reason you keep talking about two years?" Two years—when I'll be finished with college. I can't believe I didn't think of that earlier.

"Well…"

Disappointment hits. "Oh. There are other things."

"No, actually," he says wryly. "But I feel stupid for letting just one thing keep me from you. Can we pretend it's a very complex issue?"

If I doubted my feelings before, I don't anymore. How can I not be head over heels for this man who's so confident he openly admits his own foibles?

"It *is* a complex issue," I assure him. "Or it would be if I was in fact a twenty-year-old student who needed a college education in order to establish myself in life and you were in a position of authority over me. But I'm not, so if that's the only thing holding you back, there's an easy solution."

"I know." He waves a hand dismissively. "I need to get over it."

"No. I'll drop out of college."

"*What?*" He leaps to his feet, then just stands there as if unsure what to do. "You can't do that!"

"Why not?" I sound very reasonable, even to myself.

"Because… because… you can't just abandon your degree." He sinks back into his chair, looking entirely flustered. I like it.

"You're still thinking about this as if I was human," I point out, getting up and crossing the space between us to make myself comfortable on his lap. He makes an instinctive sound of protest but doesn't try to push me away. I pick up his hand and weave our fingers together. "I don't need a college degree, Rob. I've spent the equivalent of literally hundreds of years of my life in study already. I'm not depending on this degree to help me get a job and support myself. The only reason I'm at college is because I thought a liberal arts degree would help me understand human culture better—and be fun. My plans for the next few decades are to establish more youth and other community outreach programs, and I don't need an English degree for that."

He studies me, his face annoyingly blank. "Why aren't you studying business or social work, then?"

I shrug. "I don't need an entire business degree— some short courses to familiarize me with Earth processes and requirements are enough, especially combined with all the experts who already work for our government. I've already done those. As for social work —what can a human course on social work teach me about working with dragons? I have that knowledge already. I'm not twenty, remember?"

"It's beginning to sink through my thick skull. So… you're really just at college for fun?"

"Mostly. I do believe that learning about human

culture through the arts will give me a better understanding of humans, but formal study isn't necessary for that. And if we're dating, I can always ask you any questions I might have. Or I can finish my degree later on, or at a different school, or online. We have options, Rob." I try to get a sense of what he's thinking. "Does that change your perspective at all?"

"A lot," he admits. "Part of me feels guilty at even the thought that you'd drop out of school because of me, but as you've so logically explained, you're not in the same situation as most students." He pauses. "Could we compromise before we make any big decisions? Let's spend, say, two weeks getting to know each other as friends. If at that stage things are going well, we can decide what steps to take next. If it turns out we're not that into each other—"

"We will be," I interrupt, and he smiles indulgently.

"I think so too, but if we're not, then we part ways with no hurt feelings and no major life changes to undo."

He has a good point, but...

"So no sex for two weeks?"

"No sex for two weeks," he confirms.

"Are you sure? I've been told I'm exceptionally gifted."

A laugh bursts from him even as his eyes darken with lust. "I have no doubt of that at all." He shifts slightly, and his hardness presses against the side of my leg. "As you can tell, I'm very eager to experience your gifts firsthand. But I don't want to fuck this up with you. It matters too much."

I lunge at him, plastering my torso against his as I scramble to straddle him and take his mouth in the hottest kiss I've ever experienced. His lips against mine, warm and soft, are all my dreams coming true, and as he responds, his tongue dueling with mine, I wonder if anything has ever felt this good.

"Dustin," he whispers, hands on my ass and mouth on my neck as we grind together. "Dustin."

Never before has the sound of my own name been so arousing.

But we have to stop. For a second, at least.

Whimpering, I draw back just enough to get his attention. "Rob." He's been pretty firm about this no-sex thing. I don't want our first time together to be over-shadowed by regret in his memories.

Sure enough, it takes only a few seconds for the fog of lust to clear from his brain. "Damn." He sighs and rests his forehead against mine. "Damn, damn, damn."

I sigh. "Yeah, that's what I thought."

"Please don't take this the wrong way," he insists. "I want you so much, I think the ache might actually kill me."

I shift slightly, rubbing up against his dick. "Oh, I know. The feeling is mutual. But it really seems to matter to you that we get to know each other first, and I want to respect that." Intellectually I do, anyway. My body is screaming at me to show my respect in a very different way.

He huffs, half a laugh and half in exasperation. "Thank you. You're amazing." He changes the angle of his head and kisses me again, a short taste only. "Go sit in the other chair before I change my mind. Please."

For a long second, I hesitate. It would be so easy to change his mind. He wants this—wants me. The only thing stopping him right now is a foolish psychological block.

The thing is, though, that I want our relationship to be long and happy. I want it to be based on lust and love and trust and respect. And those last two items won't be there if I can't give him these two weeks.

I reluctantly get off his lap and throw myself back into the other armchair, then wince and adjust myself. Dramatic gestures are all well and good, but sometimes there are physical limitations.

He rubs the back of his neck and blows out a breath. "Just so you know, you're insanely hot."

"I know."

He shouts with laughter. "Modesty is not one of your gifts, I take it."

I love seeing him happy. "It's not immodest to acknowledge the truth. You're also insanely hot. That's why I did so badly in your classes."

Now he frowns, and I feel a pang at losing that smile. "You didn't do badly. Am I remembering wrong? I'm sure I'd remember if you'd done badly."

"I did worse than I should have. It was so hard to concentrate in class. You might have noticed that I spent a lot of time admiring your eyebrows."

Those same eyebrows rise. "My... eyebrows? Is that a euphemism?"

I shake my head. "No. I admired everything else as well, *believe* me, but I worked out that your eyebrows were the least distracting body part, so I tried to concentrate on them. They're very nicely shaped, by the way."

"Uh... thank you. That makes the time I spend grooming them worthwhile." His cheeks turn pink, and he clasps his hands together. "I'm, um, not too... boring for you? I've been called staid before. And you're… well, you're definitely not staid."

Is he insecure? About me? Delight wells up inside me. Not that he's feeling insecure, but that he's already so invested in us being together.

"I'm not staid," I admit, grateful nobody else is here to hear this. They'd be rolling on the floor laughing at the very idea of me being staid. "But I don't think you're boring. I've seen how fired up you get in class. Nobody who feels that passionately about anything could possibly be boring."

"Even though it's books and stodgy old authors?"

I snort. "Aren't you the one who taught me that Shakespeare was far from stodgy in his day?"

"True," he says, but he seems unconvinced.

"And would I be willing to hold off on sex for two weeks for someone whose company I didn't enjoy?"

"You've barely spent any time in my company," he points out.

"Maybe not, but the time we have spent together was exciting enough that I want more. Are we really going to argue about this?"

He chuckles. "No. Sorry, I didn't mean to be needy."

The word stirs something in me I didn't even know existed. "I think I like it." I lick my lips. "Sometimes. Most of the time, I'm going to be the needy one in our relationship."

Clearing his throat, he says, "That works for me."

We stare at each other, lust thick in the air. I drag my gaze away and say, "So… kissing. Can there be kisses while we get to know each other? Friends kiss, right?" Do I sound pathetically eager? Maybe because I am.

"Not the kind of kissing you're thinking of."

He's probably right. I don't think I could kiss Rob the same way I would, say, Fabian. Not that I'd kiss Fabian. We did that once, about a thousand years ago, and it scratched the itch but not much else. Any kissing between us now is purely platonic, and that's *not* how I want to kiss Rob.

I heave a huge sigh so he'll know what a sacrifice I'm making. "I guess you'd better finish setting your conditions, then."

The smile he gives me is so warm and indulgent, I want to crawl right back into his lap.

"I think we can leave it the way it is. Two weeks getting to know each other, no sex or inappropriate touching—or kissing. At school we behave as we always have. How does that sound?"

"Excruciating, but I'm up for the challenge. How are we going to get to know each other? Phone calls? Meals out? Can I visit you at your home?" I want to cram as much time with him as possible into these weeks, but I might have to give up some sleep to make this work, what with my classwork, my new commitment to the youth center project, and the travel time between here and school. Rob's totally worth it, but it's going to be a bit of a juggling act. Of course, when the two weeks are up and we agree to make this more permanent, I'll be dropping school anyway, so I might not need to worry too much about classwork right now.

"Yes to all those, as long as you think we can keep our hands off each other at my house." He seems a bit dubious about the likelihood of that. Can't say I blame him. Luckily, I have a solution.

"What about if I bring Fabian when I come to your place? You have books, I bet. He'll happily sit and read anywhere while we talk—like an old-fashioned chaperone. I can be the virtuous maiden, and you'll be the wicked seducer who'd like to get under my skirt but is thwarted by the constant presence of my loyal chaperone."

"I somehow think it would be the other way around," he says dryly, though there's a spark in his eye that makes me think he'd be open to a bit of role-playing. I make a mental note to start shopping for costumes online. "That's a good idea, though. If Fabian doesn't mind." He hesitates. "Is he always so…"

"Cluelessly weird?" I supply. I adore Fabian—we've been friends for a long time—but there's no denying the truth. "He lives in his own head a lot. But he's got incredible pickup skills. If you ever need to hook up, he's the best wingm—" I snap my mouth shut, realizing what I'm saying and to whom. I glare at him. "Not that you'll need the assistance of a wingman anytime soon, since your only options are celibacy or me." I pause to consider. "Or a threesome with Keanu Reeves."

"Keanu Reeves?" He sounds intrigued by that. I wonder if there's a way to arrange it.

Probably not.

"In my fantasies, he's always willing to play with us both."

That pink is back in his cheeks. "You've fantasized about us? And Keanu?"

"All the time," I assure him. "I haven't had sex with anyone since I started college"—he knows that already, thanks to my family's big mouths—"but I have an excellent relationship with my hand and my imagination. You get me off at least four times a week. Sometimes Keanu joins us."

He swallows hard. "Tell me about one of these fantasies." The words seem to have been dragged from him, but he doesn't take them back.

"Are you sure?" I tease. "Some of them are pretty dirty." Downright obscene, actually. When I'm particularly stressed, intense sex is the best way for me to relax.

"Start—" His voice breaks, and he tries again. "Start with a mild one."

"Hmm, okay." A mild one. Oooh, I know. "So, we live in… olden times. I don't know when. I thought of this after watching *Pirates of the Caribbean*."

He swallows hard.

"And I'm a virtuous young man of good family who's very sheltered."

His lips twitch. "You?"

"Do you want to be part of this fantasy or not? Because I can go up to my room and imagine Keanu instead."

"You know that it was Johnny Depp in *Pirates of the Caribbean*, right?"

I roll my eyes. "Duh. But he doesn't get me going like Keanu does. And you," I add. "You get me going just as much as Keanu." More, actually.

He shoots me a doubting look. "Uh-huh. So… you were being virtuous."

Right, back to the fantasy. "Yes. I'm reading a book in the garden of my wealthy father's manor house, like the quiet, good boy I am. It's a boring book about people being good and boring. My chaperone is knitting in a chair beside me."

He raises an eyebrow. "You have a chaperone?"

All this interrupting is getting old fast. How can I

build the sexual tension if he keeps breaking in? "Of course I have a chaperone. I'm a sheltered innocent."

"No, I got that bit. What I mean is, why do you need a chaperone to sit in the garden at your own home?"

I open my mouth to retort indignantly… but I've got nothing. "You're missing the point," I declare. "The chaperone goes into the house to get more knitting stuff. But she's just inside, still within earshot. And before she goes, she warns me to be a good boy. And I am a good boy, but sometimes at night, I have naughty dreams I don't really understand."

His indulgent smile fades.

"I'm all alone in the garden, reading, when I hear a noise. I assume it's the gardener and pay no attention. A few moments later, I feel a presence by my side and look up to see a stranger. A pirate." I pause. "*You.*"

Rob draws in a deep breath.

"I open my mouth to shout, but you have your hand over it already. You snatch me up out of my chair and steal me away, leaving my book as the only evidence I was ever there. I struggle, but you just laugh and call me feisty. You take me to your ship and lock me in your cabin. I'm there alone for hours, wondering what you want with me. I've been told to always stay away from pirates because they'll ravage me, but I don't really know what that means.

"And then you come back."

"What—" It comes out on a croak, and Rob clears his throat. "What do I do then?"

I'm half-hard already, since my mind and body are very familiar with this fantasy and what happens next, but the sound of Rob's voice is like an electric jolt straight to my dick. I suck in air through my nose.

"You tell me I'm pretty. That you've been watching me, and now I'm yours. Yours to play with. That I'm here to serve your pleasure. Then you order me to strip.

"I hesitate, because I haven't been naked before anyone else since I was a small child. But you're staring at me with your hot eyes, and I find myself obeying. Piece by piece, I remove my clothing, feeling more and more exposed, more and more vulnerable. Your gaze is all over me, and I find myself aroused… even though I know I shouldn't be. It's wrong. Those feelings should be reserved for my future husband."

I press down on my erection with the heel of my hand, and Rob's eyes drop to my lap, then rise to lock with mine. I don't need to look to know he's hard too.

"You undress too, and I can't look away from your big, hard cock. I've never seen anyone else's before, and I don't understand my sudden urge to kiss it. You come closer and touch me, your hands on my naked torso, and I protest. I know this is wrong. But you laugh and tell me you can do whatever you want to me, because I belong to you now.

"And then you put your hands on my shoulders and push me down to my knees."

Rob shifts in his chair, adjusting himself as I stroke my dick through my pants. This might be a mistake— might leave us both hard and aching without recourse— but it's a real thrill to share even this level of intimacy with him.

"Your cock is so hard, right in front of my face, a drop of precum welling at the tip. You put your hand on the back of my head and urge me forward, but I resist. Even though I really, really want to taste that drop of moisture, the good boy I've been raised to be knows I should be fighting this. So you rub your fat dick along my cheek and tell me you love my spirit, but you'll have me in the end. I'll beg to suck you, beg to be fucked by you. I don't know what that word means, and when I ask, your voice goes all growly. 'It means I'm going to plunder your hole,' you tell me, and even though I still don't fully understand, my hole twitches. You must see my reaction in my expression, because your tone turns coaxing. Just one lick, you tell me, and if I really don't like it, you won't make me. You'll let me put my clothes back on.

"I agree, because compromise is important, and what harm can a single lick do? I stick out my tongue and lap up the precum smeared over the head of your cock. One lick. But it's not enough. The taste of you is better than the finest wine, and I desperately want more. So I lick again, but of course there's no more precum… just the hot, musky taste of you.

"If I want more, you say, I'll have to work for it. I'll have to suck it out of you. And I know it's wrong, know that crosses a line, but I want it. The good boy is being drowned out by the boy who has secret, naughty dreams at night, and the naughty boy wants to find out what it means to be plundered. So I wrap my lips around your cockhead and suck. It's awkward at first, and you need to give me directions, but I love it. And when you put your hand on the back of my head and push your thick dick down my throat, I know there's nothing I want more than to choke on it. I let you use my mouth, alternating between sucking and letting you fuck my face, until you explode, shooting streams of your delicious essence into my mouth, and I get to swallow it all down.

"And just when I think it's over and I'm struggling

with the disappointment, you pull me to my feet, drag me to the bed, and say, 'We've only just begun.'"

I stop talking and swallow, my throat dry. The silence is broken only by our heavy breathing, and I really, really wish I could cross the space between us, go to my knees, and act out my fantasy. But I made a promise. Two weeks.

Rob exhales hard. "Wow."

I smile. Two weeks. Then I get to make him say that again.

CHAPTER NINE

Rob

I'M NOT A WILDLY popular guy. Don't get me wrong, I have friends, but I'm not the kind of person whose phone is constantly buzzing. So I've never worried about turning it off or even switching it to silent mode during class. I might occasionally get a text while I'm teaching, but I ignore it, and most of my students don't even notice. Calls? It's never happened in twenty years of teaching. People who are likely to call me know I teach during business hours and just don't try in that time.

Of course, all that was before Dustin entered my life.

The day after we came to our dating agreement (and he blew my mind, sexually, without even touching me), I wake to a text message.

Dustin: *Good morning! Hope you slept well. Loved talking to you before bed last night <3 Have a great day and see you tonight! Xx*

It made me smile, so I texted him back.

Rob: *Talking to you last night gave me the sweetest dreams. Look forward to seeing you later.*

I got a string of emojis in return, which I didn't know quite what to do with. They all involved hearts of some kind, so I guess it was good?

Half an hour later, he texted me a photo of a plate of blueberry pancakes and syrup with the caption *Kethe makes the best b'fasts! When the 2 wks is up, u'll have to stay over and try them.*

The thought of staying over with Dustin and seeing him all warm and sleep-mussed in the morning gave me an inconvenient boner, but I dutifully took a picture of my toast and sent it back. Isn't that what you're supposed to do? He sent back a sad face, so either I did it wrong or he was giving his opinion of my breakfast.

He texted me five more times on his drive to campus —thankfully Fabian was behind the wheel—and then there was a reprieve when his class began. I figured I was safe during work hours.

Boy, was I wrong.

The first text comes as my senior creative writing class is sharing their work on opening paragraphs. It's a gentle ding and discreet buzz in my pocket, so I ignore it, and so does the class, aside from one student glancing up and another making an aborted grab toward her pocket.

Two minutes later, there's another ding. Then two more in quick succession. The student who was reading falters, and most of the class is now looking up, wondering who's the asshole who didn't turn off their phone.

So of course that's when there's a flurry of dinging from my pocket.

I smile weakly. "Whoops. Bad teacher. I'm so sorry

—let me just make sure it's not an emergency." I yank out my phone and scan the screen.

Dustin: *Hi!*

Dustin: *I'm sooooo bored*

Dustin: *Prof Keating isn't as good a teacher as you*

Dustin: *Who knew it was possible to make folklore about vampires boring?*

Dustin: *Fake vampires, I mean. The human legend kind. Not the real ones.*

Dustin: *LOL imagine if I invited a real vampire to class.*

Dustin: *That would liven things up!*

Dustin: *Just sitting here thinking of you*

That last message pops up as I'm reading the others, and as touched as I am by it, I force myself not to reply. Instead, I turn off the phone and return my attention to my students.

"Sorry about that. Who was next?"

Monday is a chaotic teaching day for me. I have back-to-back classes from eight until two, so by the time I make it back to my office—after a quick stop to pick up a sandwich—my brain is mush.

I dump my bag and sandwich and slump into my desk chair, sighing. In just a second, I'm going to turn my phone back on. I have no doubt there's a flood of messages from Dustin. Hopefully he's not mad that I haven't replied. Also hopefully, I'll think of a way to tell him not to text me so much during the workday.

Although part of me doesn't want to do that. If he doesn't mind that I can't answer right away, is it really such a bad thing that he texts me? I like the idea of being able to check my phone during breaks and seeing messages from him. It gives me a warm feeling to know he's thinking of me.

Even if I should probably encourage him to concentrate on his classes more. Especially with that windbag Keating, who's the only person I know that can make fascinating subject matter dull. Unfortunately for his students, when it comes to final exams, he likes to sneak in questions on things that he skims over in class. Anyone not paying attention definitely pays the price later.

Pushing aside the dilemma of what to tell Dustin, I unwrap my sandwich and take a bite while waiting for my phone to power on.

Then nearly choke when it goes insane with text alerts.

One glance at the screen has me regretting many of my life choices.

107 new messages

Surely they can't all be from Dustin? Has something happened? Are people trying to get in touch with me due to an emergency?

No… they would have called the school when they couldn't reach me on my cell. The English department administrative staff are excellent about taking messages and finding people when necessary.

I put down my sandwich and reach cautiously for my phone.

Okay. Okay. Only some of those messages are from Dustin. Three other people have also texted me repeatedly. I have a sneaking suspicion that they may be dragons, just based on my interaction with them yesterday.

Dustin first.

I tap on his message thread and scroll through.

Dustin: *oops just realized ur prob in class*

Dustin: *sorry!*

Dustin: *But ur phone is prob off, so I'll keep txting*

Dustin: *that way, u'll have a nice surprise later!*

Dustin: *I hope it's a nice surprise*

Dustin: *No, it is. I'm delightful*

Dustin: *bet ur smiling as u read these*

Dustin: *I make ppl smile*

Dustin: *I can make u smile in a very special way*

Dustin: *yeah, that's right ;-)*

Dustin: *r u hard thinking about me?*

Dustin: *I'm getting hard*

Dustin: *not good in the middle of class*

Dustin: *lol for 2 yrs u made me hard in ur class and now ur making me hard in other classes too!*

Dustin: *ew what if Keating thinks I'm hard for him?*

Dustin: *it's all 4 u, Rob. My dick is urs*

Dustin: *wait is that weird?*

Dustin: *let's talk about other things so I don't accidentally cum in class*

Dustin: *not that I cum prematurely*

Dustin: *my stamina is legendary*

Dustin: *day-long Dustin, they call me*

Dustin: *not really but they should*

Dustin: *stop talking about sex!*

Dustin: *jsyk I gave ur number to Fabian, Sophie, and Stef*

Dustin: *Fabian wants to talk about literature I think*

Dustin: *Sophie just likes talking to ppl.*

Dustin: *but she asks a lot of invasive personal questions*

Dustin: *it's the healer in her. You can refuse to answer. She's fine with it*

Dustin: *not sure what Stef wanted.*

Dustin: *Maybe permission to do a security check on ur house*

Dustin: *u can tell him no*

Dustin: *but he's rly good at his job*

Dustin: *just a bit weird*

Dustin: *It's so easy to talk 2 u*

Dustin: *there's a real connection between us*

Dustin: *I could keep chatting with u all day*

Dustin: *can't wait 2 c u 2nite*

Dustin: *the restaurant looks rly nice*

Dustin: *private*

Dustin: *lots of chances to feel each other up under the table*

Dustin: *except we're not supposed to do that*

Dustin: *so try not to think about what it would be like*

Dustin: *me, sliding my foot up ur leg*

Dustin: *or my hand up ur thigh*

Dustin: *unzipping ur pants*

Dustin: *sliding inside*

Dustin: *do u wear boxers or briefs?*

Dustin: *I'd find out*

Dustin: *ugh, this is not helping my hard-on*

Dustin: *be back later. I need to cool off.*

I swallow hard and clear my throat, all too easily picturing Dustin fondling me at one of my favorite restaurants. Grabbing my water bottle, I chug. It's a good thing I waited until I got back here to check messages instead of doing it during one of my classes. There's no way I would have been able to concentrate after that, no matter how much I love my job.

Grabbing my sandwich, I eat half of it before checking the rest of the messages. Knowing dragons even as little as I do, I'm sure it's safer not to be chewing when reading messages from them. And I have no doubt the remaining fifty-something messages are mostly from dragons.

I open the next thread.

Unknown Number: *Hey Rob, this is Sophie! I hope you're*

having a great day. Just wanted to say hello and get to know you better. You're part of the family now! jk but not really.

Sophie: *anyhoo, is there any chance I could get a copy of your medical history? And maybe do an exam? I'm learning about human physiology, and a real human to practice on would be great!*

Sophie: *Not that I'll practice any surgical procedures or anything. Strictly nonsurgical*

Sophie: *Unless you'd be okay with it?*

Sophie: *Just basic exploratory surgery. I could probably find a human surgeon to oversee it.*

Sophie: *Let me know, and I'll start looking.*

Sophie: *Also, Fabian tells me that humans ejaculate during sex like other non-dragon species. I would very much like some samples.*

Sophie: *If you're uncomfortable with a specimen cup, don't worry. I can just harvest a sample from Dustin after you've been together.*

Sophie: *With your permission, of course. Or Dustin's. Do I need both? This might be an ethical quandary.*

Sophie: *Are you and Dustin really not having sex for two weeks? Is this a human thing? Is it related to a medical or psychological condition?*

Sophie: *I'm so excited to have a human in the family. Look forward to hearing back from you! xx*

I push away the rest of my sandwich, suddenly not hungry, and make a mental note not to let Sophie anywhere near me with anything sharp. Also, when Dustin and I start having sex, it will be at my place, and I'm making him wash thoroughly before he goes home.

Although… if she's fascinated by the fact that "non-dragon species" ejaculate, does that mean dragons don't?

How is that possible? What happens when they

orgasm? Do they come rainbows or something? And how would they procreate if there's no cum?

So many questions. I'm not asking Dustin, though—at least not yet. He'd probably offer to demonstrate, and that wouldn't be good for my self-control.

I have some more water. There are still a ton of messages to go, and if they're from Fabian and/or Steffen, I'm going to need fortitude.

Unknown Number: *Hello, Rob, this is Fabian Draco. Dustin gave me your number. I'd like to discuss nineteenth century literature with you. Please send me a message when you have time.*

Fabian: *Hello, Rob, it's Fabian again. It occurred to me that it might be more convenient for me to send you a list of questions for you to review at your leisure. The following text messages will be questions. Each message will be about a specific book. Thank you for your time.*

Fifteen messages follow, each one headed by a book title and then containing about half a dozen questions. I skim through them, impressed by how acutely he pins down each book's central themes—but then, he is an academic with years of study behind him. There are only a few weird questions, and they can be put down to lack of knowledge about humanity and human history.

I text him back quickly, asking for an email address to send detailed answers to, then move on to the final unread text thread. Fabian's was quite normal, so I've been lulled into a false sense of security.

Unknown Number: *Your number was given to me by a mutual friend. We met twice on the weekend. Is your phone secure?*

Yeeeeeaaaaahhh... this can only be Steffen. Who else would be so careful to not use names? I add him to my contacts.

Steffen: *If you're not certain your phone is secure, don't use any identifying details.*

Steffen: *I can secure your phone next time we meet. I also need to secure your house, but I don't know where it is.*

Steffen: *DO NOT TEXT ME THE ADDRESS*

Steffen: *I'll find you.*

Steffen: *Are you taking precautions when you travel between home and work?*

What follows is message after message of increasingly paranoid instructions. I scan over them, impressed by the depth of the potential conspiracy theories he comes up with. I mean, I'm sure he should be seeing a professional, but I don't know if dragons have mental health specialists? And he can't see a human—too much chance of exposure. If there's one thing I've learned from being Julian's stepson for nearly forty years, it's that exposure would be catastrophic.

I spend far too long composing a reply text that mentions no names, places, or times but assures him he can secure my phone when next we see each other. I deliberately don't mention him securing my house. I want to talk to Dustin—and maybe Brandt—about that first. If it's necessary to ensure Dustin's safety, then I'm okay with it, but otherwise, no.

Flipping back to Dustin's texts, I read them again, unable to keep from smiling. He's not really sticking to the "friends only" thing, but I can't be mad. I love how uninhibited and confident he is.

I'm still typing my reply when a new message pops up from him.

Dustin: *yay! ur back!*

Dustin: *hope ur having a great day!*

I blink at the screen, wondering how he knew I was

reading his texts, then realize he must have seen the dots while I typed. I can't resist a mildly flirtatious message back.

Me: *Yes to the great day. Although your messages have made it *harder* ;-)*

Dustin: *image*

My jaw drops as I stare at the picture filling my screen, and my cock goes from mildly interested to hard as a pike in a split second. It's a dick pic, but not the traditional kind. In fact, one could almost argue that it was an accidental photo. I know better, of course.

The shadowy image of Dustin's lap has obviously been taken in a lecture theater. He's wearing shorts, but not underwear—I can tell because the hard length of his dick is clearly outlined where it stretches along his thigh. The fabric of his shorts strains lovingly over it, displaying so much detail, he might as well be naked.

I swallow hard.

Dustin: *harder like this?*

Me: *what class are you in right now?*

And what are they talking about that's turned him on like that?

Dustin: *Technical writing. So boring. But just thinking of u does this to me.*

I have a sneaking suspicion I'm not going to last two weeks.

CHAPTER TEN

Dustin

"This'll just take a minute," I promise Fabian. "Just lean against the wall next to the open door so everything looks innocent if someone walks by."

He frowns. "I thought everything *was* innocent? You've still got eight days left on the no-humping agreement."

I cringe. "Can you not call it that? Or not in front of Rob, anyway."

Fabian glances in confusion around the corridor we're walking down. "We're not in front of Rob. So are you going to do something not-innocent in his office? You promised him two weeks, Dustin. It might have been a stupid agreement, but it's still an agreement."

"I *know*. Believe me, I know." I especially know when I jerk myself to sleep every night while thinking of him. "I'm not going to do anything that will break our agreement. I'm just going to talk to him. But I'm bringing you to be an extra layer of innocence."

Fabian doesn't look convinced, but we're at Rob's office now, so it's too late for him to argue. I take a second to absorb how hot he looks sitting behind his desk, typing something and studying the screen with a sexy little furrow between his brows, then knock lightly on the open door.

He glances up, and for a split second, his whole face lights up with joy, filling me with all kinds of warmth. Then his eyes widen.

"Hey, Professor," I say quickly before he can panic. "Fabian and I just thought we'd stop by and let you know we have to go back home tonight. I sent you a text, but I know you keep your phone off during the day." That's because I love to text him, and he says he doesn't have the willpower to keep from checking his phone if he thinks it might be me.

He's on his feet and halfway around his desk before I finish speaking. "Is everything okay?"

I nod, taking a step back so I don't accidentally leap into his arms. "Yeah, just Steffen wants to do a security review." I roll my eyes. "We've been putting him off for a while, and he's getting antsy, so Grandfather said we'll do it tonight when he and Percy get back from the city." I try not to show how peeved I am to be missing out on this Friday night with Rob. I'd invite him to join us, but Stef might lose his mind if an "unauthorized" person was at the meeting. "Are we still on for tomorrow?"

Out in the hallway, Fabian begins coughing loudly. He's a terrible actor, so it's obvious he's faking it. Rob and I both turn toward the doorway, and a second later, Professor Yang appears.

Fuck. Did he hear me confirming plans with Rob?

"Hey, Gerald," Rob says calmly. "I'll just be a minute."

"Hi, Professor Yang," I add, trying to be casual.

"Hello, Dustin. I can wait while you finish up." He leans against the doorframe, seemingly unconcerned, but there's something in his face that makes my heart race with worry. Thank fuck Rob and I weren't touching when he came in—there was about three feet of space between us. But did it look odd for Rob to be standing near me instead of sitting in his desk chair?

"I think that's it, thanks, Professor," I say to Rob. "If you're okay with reading my short story, I can bring it to you tomorrow. Or email it," I add. Am I adding too many details? I used to be such a good prevaricator, but love seems to have scrambled my brains.

"Email is fine," Rob agrees. He doesn't add anything more, and I know he's hating this. My stomach sinks. I never wanted him to have to go through this— the secrecy and the lies. I would gladly quit school to save him from it, but how would that help in this situation? Can you imagine how bad it would be if I turned to Professor Yang right now and said, "I'll quit college so Rob and I can be together without breaking the rules"? For one, it would be an admission that something is going on between us. And right now, that's not technically true. No-humping friend agreement, remember?

Trying to keep my wits around me, I smile. "Thanks again. See you later, Professor Yang."

They both say goodbye, and I leave as quickly as I can without running.

In the hallway, Fabian stares at me with wide eyes, his mouth opening, but I hold a finger to my lips. "Thanks for waiting, Fabian. We can go now."

Thankfully, he catches on. "Great. Uh, can we stop for tacos?"

"Tacos?" I mouth, pulling a what-the-fuck face. He shrugs.

"Sure." I release a slow stream of magic, creating the sound of footsteps fading down the hallway. Then Fabian and I huddle against the wall. I really hope nobody comes by, because we look suspicious as fuck.

"Jesus, Rob, what are you doing?" Professor Yang demands. "I know I joked about this, but—"

"I'm not doing anything," Rob interrupts sharply. "There's nothing untoward between me and Dustin."

Professor Yang scoffs. "Please. I might not have caught you actually doing anything, but that kid can't lie for shit."

Hey! Indignation swamps me, and I barely hold back from storming into the office and telling him I'm an excellent liar.

"Not to mention," he continues, "that he's barely been able to look you in the eye without blushing and stammering for two years, but now he's so confident he's coming to… what was it? *Ask you to read a short story.* Which he was apparently going to bring to you on a Saturday. Please."

Rob makes a frustrated sound. "I know it looks bad, Gerald, but there really is nothing like that going on. It turns out that Dustin's family is acquainted with my stepfather, and I ran into him at a party at my parents' house last weekend. I can't explain why that made him relax around me—maybe seeing me outside the class-room setting helped him get over his crush."

There's a faint tremor in Rob's voice on the last sentence, and my chest aches. This is my fault. I never should have come here today and forced him into having to lie to his friend. I'd already sent him a text, and I could have called later, but no, I was so desperate to see him, just for a minute, that I caused this whole awful situation that he wanted so badly to avoid.

"Fine." Professor Yang's tone clearly says he doesn't believe a word of it. "I'm only saying this because I'm your friend and I don't want to see you throw your career away. I thought his crush was sweet and amusing when I knew nothing would happen between you, but—"

I grab Fabian's hand and pull him silently down the hall, with the help of a bit of magic to muffle our steps, and don't stop until we're outside again.

I'm shaking.

"Dustin?" Fabian puts an arm around me and steers me to a nearby raised garden bed with a handy retaining wall for me to sit on. "Take a deep breath."

I obey, sucking air deeply into my lungs and then devolving into a coughing fit. Guess my lungs don't want that much air.

"Are you okay?" a new voice asks, and I look up as Zara joins us. Great. As much as I adore her, I've been avoiding her all week. Well, avoiding her outside of class. She probably won't be able to tell that my life has changed, but what if she somehow guesses?

"Fine," I choke out between wheezes.

"He swallowed a bug," Fabian says.

Zara raises a brow. "Really? Because it looked to me like he was about to faint or something and you made him sit down."

"Right," Fabian agrees. "And that's when he swallowed the bug." He blinks innocently at her.

She shakes her head, then pushes him aside and sits beside me on the retaining wall. "Clear the remnants of bug juice from your throat and tell me what's wrong," she orders.

"Nothing's wrong," I tell her, my voice almost normal.

"I don't believe you."

"Uh, since you're not going to pass out and hit your head anymore, I'm going to go to my last class," Fabian says, looking distractedly in the direction of the history and arts building.

I flip my hand at him. "Go. I'm fine."

He goes.

"Now that he's gone, you can tell me what the problem is," Zara insists.

"Don't you have class too?" My desperation is audible, and I wince.

"Nope," she announces cheerfully. "I have plenty of time to sit here with you and hear all about whatever it is that just freaked you out."

"I'm not— Fine." I give in at the disbelieving look on her face. "Fine, you're right. I'm... somewhat upset right now. But it's not the end of the world, and I don't need looking after." I really hope it's not the end of *my* world. I don't know what I'll do if this convinces Rob to back away from taking a chance on us.

"I thought we were friends," she says, and the bossiness is gone, replaced by hurt. I close my eyes.

"We are friends," I protest weakly. "I... look, can you keep a secret?" I weigh things up quickly. While I honestly believe Zara is trustworthy, even if she's not, what's the most harm she can do? If Rob and I stay together, I'll be quitting school and there won't be anything for people to hold against him. If we don't, well, I'll probably still be quitting school. For one thing, I don't think I could handle being on the same campus and knowing he doesn't want me. For another, Julian was very impressed by my written proposal for the youth outreach center. He only wanted to make a few tweaks before sending it to Lihua Jiǎng. She's already replied that she likes the look of it but is waiting for her accountant and lawyer to weigh in. It's not a definite yes, but things are looking very positive. Getting the program off the ground and running it would be a full-time job, at least initially, and by the time it's in a place to be handed over to someone else to run, I'll be looking at expanding. So finishing an English degree is not at the top of my priority list right now.

Zara looks me dead in the eye. "I swear I can."

I glance around to make sure nobody's close enough to overhear, then lower my voice. "Last weekend, I went with my grandfather to a fundraising party." I carefully pick and choose which details I can tell her. She already thinks I'm planning to go to work for "the family business," and that my degree is just for fun. Which is mostly true. So I can play that up to my advantage. "I've been thinking lately that I don't want to be here for another two years on the same campus as Rob, and—"

"Wait, who's Rob?" Her jaw drops. "Do you mean Professor Sarris? Did you finally make a move?"

"Shh," I hiss, although her voice was already barely above a whisper. "Not exactly. Well, yes. But let me explain. He was at the party—his parents were the hosts. I got to talk to him a bit and kind of threw myself at him."

"You were actually able to talk to him? No stuttering?" she asks doubtfully.

"You've missed the point." Although, given how I

used to behave around Rob, I can't really blame her. "I threw myself at him."

"And he went for it?" Her shock is clear.

I shake my head. "No. He said he'd never cross that line with a student."

She puts her hand over her heart. "I know that's not the outcome you wanted, but he's such a good guy. So principled and upstanding."

I glare at her. "Stop fantasizing about him."

A laugh escapes her while she rolls her eyes. "Lesbian, remember? I can appreciate a man's moral fiber without wanting the man himself."

Not entirely convinced, I grumble, and she puts an arm around me.

"I'm so sorry he rejected you, though. I'm sure it was a really hard decision for him to make. Is this why you've been weird all week?"

I swallow hard. Crunch time. "Kind of? Uh, he didn't… I mean, he did reject me, but then I told him my degree wasn't essential for my future and about how I'm going to work for Grandfather and could happily drop out anytime, and—"

"Dustin! Are you…" She trails off and looks around carefully. When she speaks again, her voice is so soft, I can barely hear her. "Are you fucking Professor Sarris?"

I lean in, so she does as well. When we're so close to each other that we're almost cross-eyed, I say, "No."

"You're such an ass." She smacks my arm and starts to get up, but I grab her hand.

"I'm not finished! Sit down." It takes me another minute to convince her, but finally she's sitting beside me again. "Anyway, I told him all that stuff, but he wasn't convinced. He doesn't want to ruin my life, and he doesn't want to risk his career."

"But he wanted you? Are you sure he wasn't just letting you down gently?"

I think back to our kiss in the garden last Saturday night and smile. "Uh, no. He definitely wants me."

Zara eyes me but doesn't ask for details. "So then what?"

"We made a bargain. Friends only for two weeks. No sex, no kissing, no behavior that couldn't be featured on a G-rated kids' show."

"And *you* agreed to this?" The doubtful tone is back. "After all the longing and angst, you agreed to be just friends?"

"For two weeks," I remind her. "If at the end of the two weeks, the attraction is still there and we have the basis for more, then I drop out of school and we get together officially."

For a long moment, she stares fixedly at me. Is she having some kind of medical crisis? Should I call for help?

"Zara? Can you hear me? Blink once if you can hear me." I wave my hand in front of her face. She slaps it aside.

"Oh my god," she gasps. "Oh my god!"

I bite my lip to keep from telling her that her god is a myth. My Earth friends counseled us all about that. Humans can apparently be very uptight about their religions, even when they think they're not.

"So you and he are… what? Courting?"

I'm so thankful for two years studying classical literature, or I wouldn't have a clue what she meant by that word. "I guess so."

"And you've changed your mind?"

"What? No! Why would you think that?"

She gestures to me. "Because you had a panic attack before, remember? Fabian practically had to hold you upright."

I shake my head. "No, that was because I think I might have done something stupid." I explain what happened in Rob's office. "And now I'm worried that he's going to back away. I mean… all his fears came true, and it's my fault." I stare glumly at the ground, pouting. It's not fair. I was so close to having it all, and a stupid mistake might take it all away.

"You're an idiot," Zara declares.

"Huh?"

"An idiot. I-D-I-O-T."

"I know how to spell it, thanks," I snap.

"Think about it. If you were planning to finish out your degree and any relationship between you was going to be all secrets and lies for another two years, then yeah, you'd be fucked. But you're not, so there's no downside to being together, if that's what he wants. I mean, he might decide he just can't stand your company," she teases, "but if he actually likes you and wants to be with you, and you're not going to be a student here… there's no barrier. What happened in his office was just a minor inconvenience."

I sit there with my mouth open, staring at her. Could she be right?

"Look, why don't you text him? Apologize for the near miss and assure him it won't happen again. If he's really that upset by it, he'll break it off with you right away."

"Do you think so?"

She shrugs. "No idea. But what would be the point in dragging it out? It's not like he's getting sex in the meantime. If you're really worried, just ask him."

I shudder. "I don't want to put the idea in his head if he's not already thinking it." But she might be right about texting him. His phone will still be off, so he won't even see it for a few more hours.

Before my courage can escape me, I pull out my cell and send a message.

Dustin: *So sorry about this afternoon. I swear I intended nothing inappropriate. Hope I haven't caused trouble for you. It won't happen again.*

I hesitate, then send another one.

Dustin: *Talk later? I'll call you after nine. Stef should be done by then.*

There. If Zara's right, I should know where I stand before I go to bed tonight.

"Thank you," I tell her. "You're a good friend."

"I try." She pats my knee. "So you're dropping out, huh?"

"It's time." I nod, trying to seem like someone eager to work in the family business. "I've really enjoyed school, but I'm keen to get to what's next. I'll miss you, though. You won't drop out of touch, will you?" I'm surprised by how much I mean it.

She grins at me. "No chance. I'm going to need to hear alllllll about your love life."

SITTING cross-legged in the middle of my bed, I stare anxiously at my phone on the mattress in front of me.

The clock on the lock screen says 8:57, and I'm waiting impatiently for it to tick over to nine o'clock so I can call Rob. He probably wouldn't care if I called a few minutes early, but after the trouble I caused this afternoon, I'm determined to prove to him that I can stick to my word. Even if it's something as small as what time I'll call.

He replied to my texts earlier, while I was in the middle of listening to Steffen blather, but the simple *talk to you then* tells me nothing about whether he's mad or planning to end things between us before they even begin.

I suck in a deep breath and for the third time check the notes I made earlier and printed out for easy reference. I'm not letting go without a fight. If Rob wants to end things because of what happened this afternoon, I have a handy list of reasons why that would be a dumb idea, thanks to my talk with Zara. Fabian had a few things to add too, in the car on the drive home. Logically, there's no reason Rob shouldn't allow our trial to finish.

The alarm on my phone blares, and I jump. Fuck. I was waiting for it, and it still scared the crap out of me. Snatching up the phone, I swipe to clear the alarm and take another deep breath.

Go time.

It takes only seconds to bring up my contacts and tap Rob's number, but it feels like it's happening in slow motion. My heartbeat thunders in my ears.

"Hi, Dustin," Rob's warm voice says, and he sounds… happy? To hear from me?

That's a good sign, right?

"I'm so sorry," I blurt. "So sorry." I stare blindly at

my list, mentally prepping a response for whatever he says next.

He chuckles. "It's fine, Dustin. You didn't do anything wrong. We just had some bad luck."

My brain freezes. "Really?" I breathe. "I mean, yes! It was just rotten luck."

"Have you been worried about this all afternoon?"

I lean back against my pillows. "Kind of. I-I was afraid you might see it as a bad sign for us. It was basically the fulfillment of all your fears."

"True," he concedes, "but those fears don't apply to our plans. Unless you've reconsidered and want to stay in school? Be honest."

"I really don't," I assure him. "Even if the funding for the outreach program doesn't come through right away, I have ideas for how to get it. And so many more plans. Whether things work between us or not, I don't think I'll be staying in school." It's the second time I've said it out loud, and it feels even more right this time. College has been a great experience for me, and I've learned a lot about human culture here, but I've gotten about as much out of it as I'm going to. Other things in my life have a higher priority now.

"Well, you still have another week to change your mind. Or anytime after that, even if it means we need to adjust our plans."

I grin. That sounds like he's already thinking of a future with me.

"So," I begin, ready to change the subject, "what are you wearing?"

He laughs. "Don't push your luck, minx. Friends only, remember?"

"I'm asking as a friend," I protest innocently. "Why

must you assume I have nefarious sexual motivations?" I totally do, but I know how far I can push his boundaries.

"Mmm, so you're interested in what I'm wearing from a fashion perspective, then?" He sounds amused and relaxed, and I love it.

"Absolutely. I'm fascinated by your personal style."

His laugh rings out again, sending warm thrills down my spine. "Well, I'm sorry to disappoint you, but I'm wearing very old, very ratty pj bottoms."

An image rises in my mind's eye of him in worn, faded pajama pants, the fabric so soft and clingy from years of use that it drapes lovingly over every inch of him, and I swallow hard. "And nothing else?" My voice is raspy, and I clear my throat.

"Dustin," he scolds. "That's not appropriate."

"No. Of course not. Sorry." I slip my hand inside my boxers and stroke my semihard cock. "Uh, I just meant I'm wearing pj's too," I lie, mentally filing those images of Rob for later use.

Or…

"So, tell me about your day," I urge, and then close my eyes and let the sound of his voice wash over me as I tease myself fully erect.

This isn't going to take long, not with Rob talking to me. I stroke in rhythm with the cadence of his words, imagining it's his hand tight around me, that those are his fingers tickling my balls as they pull up tight. My thumb glances over the head of my cock, and I remember my pirate fantasy. Remember Rob's face as I told him I wanted him to put me on my knees and fuck my face. My breath catches, and I stroke faster, then clench my teeth to keep my cry in as I come.

"Are you done yet?" Rob asks softly, breaking into my afterglow.

Uh-oh.

He can't possibly mean…?

Can he?

"Done what?" I ask, trying to sound like I don't know what he's talking about.

"Done jerking off."

"Uh—"

"It was fine this time, Dustin, since you had a rough afternoon. But not again. Please respect the conditions we set."

The stern words and tone send a shiver down my spine and cause my spent cock to stir with interest. "I'm sorry?" It comes out sounding like a question, so I try again. "I really am sorry for not waiting until later. I know you want all our interactions to be sex-free."

"For the next week, at least," he mutters, but before I can get too excited, he adds, "This time is supposed to give any future relationship we have a strong foundation."

"I know, and I want that too. Which is why I'll only say one more thing about it, and then we can go back to being strictly friends."

"What thing?" he asks warily.

"When our relationship becomes sexual, I want you to read to me while watching me jack myself. And then I'll suck you off."

He coughs.

"Any book in particular?"

It's just as well he can't see my smile, because it feels wholly smug. "Your choice. Make it something boring so we can prolong the experience."

CHAPTER ELEVEN

Rob

DESPITE THE ALMOST-PROBLEM in my office last week, things are going so well between me and Dustin that I'm not prepared for drama to come from another source.

It's late Thursday afternoon. I've just gotten home from work, have sneaked out a bit early to cook something special, and I'm expecting Dustin within the hour. And Fabian, of course. Part of me is really regretting the whole chaperone thing, but on the flip side, with sex off the table, Dustin and I have talked a lot and really gotten to know each other. This time together wasn't a mistake. I already knew he was intelligent and thoughtful in addition to being sexy and attractive, but there's so much more to him than even that. While Fabian loses himself in my books, often needing to be physically shaken to get his attention, Dustin and I have shared parts of ourselves that rarely see the light of day. He's spoken about his "misspent youth" and how he's been trying for a long time now to get his grandfather's attention.

"I went about it the wrong way," he admitted. "I

thought he'd see me being frivolous and try to drag me into his work to keep me on the straight and narrow. Instead, I just convinced him that I was completely irresponsible. But I'm fixing that."

He's told me about his goals for building better programs and systems to support his community, about how acting as a liaison during the migration opened his eyes to all the things people are missing out on without even realizing they need them. He's focused and passionate and caring in a way that seems like a huge contrast to the flirty, almost frivolous part of him but actually works in beautiful balance. He's so easy to talk to, and I've found myself sharing lots of not-so-easy memories from when I was a kid that I don't talk about, ever. My mom is amazing and did an incredible job raising me, but back then, people weren't always so accepting of the fact that she was proudly single and I didn't have a dad. Nobody dared sneer at Mom—not more than once, anyway—but when she wasn't around, I was often an unfortunate target. Dustin's experience of losing his parents when he was very young was different, partly because of Brandt, but also because of Dustin's personality. He's a lot like my mom in the way he takes on the world, whereas I prefer to engage only when I'm comfortable. We complement each other that way.

So things are going well. Really well. In three days, our two weeks will officially be up, and I can't wait. Which is why I'm in a great mood when my phone rings and I see my stepdad's name on the screen.

I swipe to answer and put it on speaker so I can continue peeling potatoes. Dustin has a weakness for french fries, so I'm making him some from scratch. "Hey, Julian."

"Rob, good." He sounds harried and distracted, and I immediately put the knife down. "Listen, you might want to call Dustin."

"What?" I reach for the phone, uncaring of the starchy potato residue I'm getting all over it. "Why? He's coming for dinner in a little while." Even as I say it, a message notification pops up on the screen.

Dustin: *i need to cancel tonight. Talk later.*

"What happened?" I ask Julian, my stomach sinking. Dustin was very vocal last weekend about his disappointment over our canceled Friday night together. He wouldn't cancel again without a reason, and it's weird that he didn't call or at least send a more detailed text.

Julian sighs. "Lihua Jiǎng declined to fund his proposal for the youth outreach center."

Crap. "Oh no." He was so excited about that center. "I'll call him now."

"Wait, Rob, there's more."

Nothing good ever came after a sentence like that. I freeze.

"What?" I ask warily.

"We got the refusal early today, and I asked one of my staff to discreetly see if they could find out why. You know, to help us target our plans better for our next attempt."

"Sure."

"Unfortunately, that staff member sent their findings to both me and Dustin."

"Julian, just come out and say it. You're freaking me out."

He sighs heavily. "Lihua's lawyer did some minor, unofficial background checking on Dustin. Apparently he heard some stories about wild exploits, and he's advised Lihua that Dustin's not a fit person to manage this kind of program."

"*What?* That's ridiculous!"

"I know," Julian assures me. "I've done my own checks on Dustin, and while he may have been a wild child, all evidence points to that being behind him. The feedback on his behavior in the past few years is all exemplary. But this guy was born with a stick up his ass, and he doesn't like that Lihua might want to invest in projects he didn't bring to her attention."

"Okay," I mutter. Fuck, this is going to hit all Dustin's buttons. "Let's leave for now the fact that you're running background checks on my boyfriend. But we'll come back to it another time."

"If he's going to be associated with my charities, I need to take those steps, Rob," Julian insists quietly. "This had nothing to do with you." He pauses. "Boyfriend?"

Whoops. "Not now, Julian. What happened after Dustin saw the… was it an email?"

"Yes," he confirms. "He called me and said he would withdraw all connection to the program and suggested I tell Lihua that and see if it changed her mind. He didn't sound like himself, Rob, and he hung up before I could convince him that wasn't necessary."

"It's not necessary?" I check. "This program is important to him, and I know he'd rather disassociate himself from it than see it fail."

"It won't fail," Julian scoffs. "I've already set up an appointment with Lihua for tomorrow to get to the bottom of this. I've known her a long time, and I can guarantee that once she knows the whole story, not just the bits her lawyer has cherry-picked to feed her, she'll be back on board. She was very enthusiastic about the program when she read the proposal, and she liked Dustin a lot."

"But if she doesn't change her mind?"

"Then I'll ask if removing Dustin would have any impact on her decision," he says reluctantly. "I don't think it will come to that. And if she still declines to offer funding, we'll just start looking at other options. Dustin's had some great ideas, and I'm looking forward to working with him on them." He sighs again. "I don't know why he's taken this so personally. Is it just because dragons are dramatic by nature?"

I clear my throat. "Partly. But this is also a thing for him. Let me talk to him, and I'll touch base with you later."

Julian agrees and says goodbye, and I just stand there in my kitchen for a second, trying to work out my best option.

First I try calling Dustin. It goes to voicemail. I don't bother sending him a text, deciding instead to call Fabian, in case they haven't left campus yet.

That goes to voicemail too.

So I call Sophie.

"I was just about to call you," she exclaims, and I blink at the phone.

"You were?"

"Dustin and Fabian just got home, and Dustin's gone to sulk in his room. Fabian doesn't know why, just that Dustin said they had to come straight home right away. Percy and Brandt aren't here, and Kethe and I aren't sure if we should be dragging him out by the hair or making him tea and cookies."

"Leave him," I tell her. "I'm on my way. Do I need

clearance from Steffen to get in?" I didn't last weekend, but who knows with Steffen.

"Nah, he's not here. We're pretty casual when he's not around. So you know what's wrong with Dustin?"

"Yes. Let him sulk a bit and bring him the tea and cookies, please. I'll be there in"—I glance at the clock as I dump the potatoes that are already peeled into a bowl and fill it with water—"less than an hour, I hope." There's going to be a little bit of traffic at this time, but it's not such an urban area that it'll be bad, and most of the drive is on the highway.

"Okay. Should I tell Kethe to bring out the Tim Tams? Or is it not that bad?"

I stop with my hand on the plate I plan to use to cover the bowl of potatoes. "Tim Tams?"

"You know, the Australian chocolate cookies. They're Dustin's favorites, but we don't have them all the time."

I have so many questions, but this isn't the time to ask them. "Give him the cookies he likes. He's had a bad day."

"Gotcha," Sophie agrees sunnily. "See you soon."

It takes me five minutes to wash my hands, grab my keys, and get out the door.

"He wouldn't let me in even when I told him I had Tim Tams," Kethe says worriedly, leading me down a hallway to Dustin's bedroom. "I've never seen him like this before. He's usually so good-natured and happy." She hesitates in front of a closed door and lowers her voice. "Should I call Brandt and have him and Percy come home?"

"No!" a muffled voice yells from inside the room, reminding me that dragon hearing is much better than mine.

Kethe sighs and knocks. "Dustin?"

"Go away!"

"Rob's here."

There's a pause.

"You're tricking me. Go away. I don't want tea and cookies. I just want to be alone." His voice shakes in a way that breaks my heart.

"Dustin, I'm really here," I call softly. "We need to talk. Please."

A moment later, the lock turns and the door opens an inch, just enough for me to see a bloodshot hazel eye peering through the gap. He gasps, opens the door wider, and yanks me inside before slamming it closed.

"I'll just go back to the kitchen, then," Kethe calls. "Let me know if you change your mind about that tea. Rob, are you staying for dinner?"

"If you don't mind," I reply.

"No trouble at all." We hear the sound of her footsteps receding up the hall, and then I turn to Dustin.

He peers miserably up at me, his eyes puffy and lip swollen from being bitten. All thoughts of scolding him for running away flee, and I open my arms.

He leaps into them, burying his face against my shoulder, and says something that's a little too muffled for me to understand.

"I missed that, honey. Say again?"

Lifting his head, he looks at me and repeats, "Did Julian call you? I fucked it all up."

"Yes, Julian called me, but you didn't fuck it up. Which you'd know if you'd answered when he tried to call you back." I look around the spacious and frankly gorgeous room, then steer him toward an oversized armchair in the corner. Settling into it, I pull him onto my lap and cuddle him close. This is breaking all our conditions, but there are extenuating circumstances.

"I did fuck it up," he insists stubbornly. "Me and my stupid flibbertigibbet past. I should have known this would happen. I should have known I could never be worth anyone's respect."

"Stop that," I snap. "That's not true. Even if you were still the same irresponsible person you used to be, you'd be worth respect." I take a deep breath and try to speak more calmly. "But your past isn't important, Dustin. Julian knows that. He knew all about your former recklessness and still wants to trust the person you are now with the reputation of his charity."

His big wet eyes stare up at me pitifully. "But he'll lose all his funding," he whispers. "I'm no good to him if people refuse to donate money because of me."

"You should have answered when he called you so he could explain. Are you listening to me now?"

He nods, chewing on his lip but the beginnings of hope shining in his gaze. I free his poor lip from its torture and rub it with my thumb while I explain what Julian told me. "So you see, there's every chance that the funding is going to come through anyway. And even if it doesn't this time, Julian still wants you. This program is your baby, and you're the perfect person to run it. He's confident that with your help, the funding can be found."

Sniffling, he considers what I've said. "So it's not ruined because of me?"

"Absolutely not."

He exhales hard and buries his face against my chest. "I've been trying so hard," he says, his voice shaking. "I know I took too long to outgrow my carefree stage, but I've been trying so hard to show people I'm not like that anymore."

I consider the best way to approach this. I hate that he feels as though he needs to disavow any part of himself. "I didn't know you then," I begin carefully, "but from what I've heard, you were never destructive. You were never cruel or hurtful. You were… exuberant. Maybe you got carried away a bit. Maybe it lasted beyond when other people thought it should have stopped. But you're a good person, Dustin, and I can't believe you were anything but a good person then, too. And lately you've proved that you have what it takes to manage this kind of thing. You're the person you are now because of your past experiences, and people are going to see that."

He's quiet for a moment, then sniffles again and nods. "I hope so. I guess we can only wait and see how Julian's meeting goes."

"Nope. Not good enough."

He blinks at me, startled. "It's not?"

"What are you going to do if, for some misguided reason, Ms. Jiǎng still decides not to fund the program?"

His mouth opens in consternation, then that stubborn expression I've gotten so used to takes over. "I'm not giving up," he declares. It's only slightly spoiled by the way he swipes his hand under his nose. I fish in my pocket and hand him a clean tissue. "Thank you," he says, then mops his face and blows his nose. "You're right. I can't just wait to see what happens. If Lihua Jiǎng decides not to fund us, I need to be ready with plans to find the money elsewhere."

I smile. *He's back.*

"You're staying for dinner, right?" he asks as he jumps off my lap and rushes over to grab his phone from the nightstand.

"I'd planned to, since we're obviously not eating at my place." I stand and then hover awkwardly.

"Sorry about that." He's already tapping away, his attention split. I love that look of determination. "But thank you for coming to remind me what matters." He glances up at me. "I needed you."

I swallow hard as something clicks in my brain. Who knew that all this time, I wanted to be needed? I think back over everything I've loved most while getting to know Dustin: the way he's always close, touching if possible. The way he focuses so completely on me while he's speaking, then lights up when I smile or praise him. I guess I love being wanted and needed. And not just needed by anybody, but by a fiercely independent man who forges his own way through life. By Dustin.

He comes over, rises on tiptoe, and kisses me firmly on the mouth. "I know that's against the rules, but I've had a bad day, so I get a freebie."

Then he unlocks the door and wanders out, shouting to Kethe that he could really use a cuppa. There's a faintly British inflection on the word, which I'm guessing he picked up from Percy. I'm grinning as I follow him. Being with him is never going to be boring.

CHAPTER TWELVE

Dustin

You know that feeling when you've achieved something amazing and you know it, but there's a tiny part of you that worries maybe you're wrong, and you actually fucked it up? That's how I feel right now, waiting for Rob to arrive. Today's the official last day of the two-week "getting to know each other" friendship trial. Rob's coming for lunch and to assess what we want to do next, just like we agreed two weeks ago.

The outcome is pretty much a foregone conclusion. Rob and I have been almost inseparable—we've spent almost every evening together, plus a few lunches and all of last weekend. That's not even mentioning the texts and phone calls. There's no doubt that we're compatible. We have so much in common, and even though we don't agree on everything (he's convinced pineapple doesn't belong on pizza, and he's *wrong*), we do on the important things. Conversation between us is never stilted. And he came to my rescue when I needed someone—needed him.

We still haven't had sex—I think I could have

persuaded him, but when I saw how close he was to giving in to temptation, I backed off. That sounds stupid, I know, but ultimately, if he really wanted it, he could have made the first move. I want him to know I respect his wishes even when I think they're ridiculous and even when I'm pushing boundaries.

So today is really just a formality. We've already made plans for things in the future, which I'm sure he wouldn't have done if he intended to tell me we couldn't be together. But there's still a tiny part of me that's worried he's going to say he doesn't think we're compatible. That he doesn't want me.

Ugh, self-doubt sucks. It's not helped by the fact that I'm emotionally bruised from what happened last Thursday. The thought that I might have endangered the youth outreach program really messed with my head. Julian says his meeting with Lihua Jiǎng on Friday went really well, but she requested the weekend to think things over before making a final decision. So... we're waiting. And honestly, it still makes me feel like shit. I know I'm capable and responsible enough to do this, and Julian has faith in me, but we're not the ones whose opinions matter right now. That means I'm vulnerable and emotional, even though I'm trying to be confident, and that vulnerability has decided to get its claws into all parts of my life. Including my relationship with Rob.

Anyway, that's why I'm pacing the front hall at Here Be Dragons. I can't concentrate on anything, and Kethe kicked me out of the kitchen after I got distracted while making tea and accidentally spilled boiling water all over the counter. I mean, it's just *water*, but she got all stroppy and made me leave. With no other way to occupy myself, I decided to wait near the front door. I would have waited near the front gate, but I didn't want to look desperate. Plus, what if he arrives while I'm still walking down? Then someone else would let him in and he might think I'm not completely invested in our relationship.

That doesn't make sense when I think about it closely, but I've committed to pacing the hall now.

"What's he doing?" Fabian whispers from behind me.

"Wearing a path in the floor," Grandfather says dryly.

"Why? The room's big, but not so big we need a fixed path to navigate through it."

Would it be so bad if I strangled my longtime friend?

Grandfather must be able to tell I'm considering it, because he sends Fabian to give a message to Kethe, then approaches me slowly.

"Dustin? Is something wrong or are these just pre-commitment nerves?"

I don't think I've ever given him such a scathing look in my life. "I'm not nervous about committing to Rob." My heart sings at the very thought.

Grandfather nods. "So these are entirely foolish nerves that he might not want to commit to you."

I turn on him. "Is it foolish?" I ask desperately. This is so unlike me, but I can't bear to think of Rob walking away.

"Very foolish," he assures me. "Even I can tell that Rob is head over heels for you. I don't fully understand what this no-sex thing was, though."

Oh. Oops. I never explained...

"Grandfather," I begin hesitantly. Last time I

mentioned dropping out of school, he did *not* take it well. That was two years ago, though, and he thought I'd regressed to my flighty old self. "One of Rob's concerns about being with me was that I'm a student at the college he teaches at." I give him some of the details and explain the solution we'd decided on. "So you see," I conclude, "if Rob wants to continue our relationship, I'll be dropping out of college."

Grandfather nods slowly, but his lips are pursed. It's his "thinking" face, the one he's been making as far back as I can remember, and I feel a rush of affection. "What will you be doing instead?"

"Well, there's the new youth outreach center," I say promptly. "It needs to be set up, and I'll be involved in running it for at least the first few months." I hope. But if not, I'll be busy looking for other funding opportunities. Plus I can get started on planning for potential new centers, because expansion is going to happen. I explain all this to Grandfather.

"Ideally, I'd like these smaller programs to be a trial run for a larger network. Starting with youth outreach in small towns, but ultimately, I think there's room for more outreach services across the entire community."

"And that's what you want to do? Provide these services?"

"Facilitate them," I correct. "I'm not the right person to provide a lot of the needed services. But I'm good at talking to people and finding out what they need and then finding a way to help them get it." There's a defiant note in my voice that I wish wasn't there. It makes me sound like a petulant child. But what I said is true—I *am* good at communicating with people, and my lifelong connection with Grandfather and King Raðulfr has taught me a lot about diplomacy and bureaucracy. I know how to work the system to get things for people. My time as the migration liaison might not have lasted long, but I did excellent work.

"You are," he agrees, and I'm not shocked, exactly, but… I guess I am a little. Part of me still expects Grandfather to see me as spoiled and flighty. "I'm not surprised this is the path you're choosing, Dustin. You've always been a giver. Maybe we should make a time to sit down and discuss your plans officially, see where I and the government can support you."

The lump in my throat is so big, I can barely breathe, but I force myself to swallow it down and choke out an agreement. "That would be excellent."

He smiles at me, so proud and loving that I blink back tears. "We'll arrange that, then. As soon as you've finished untangling yourself from the college."

The gate buzzer goes off before I can reply, and I realize with some shock that I'd forgotten to be nervous about Rob's arrival. It all comes flooding back, and I freeze.

"I'll just get that, shall I?" Grandfather says when I don't move. He moves over to the control panel and presses a button. "Hi, Rob. The gate's opening."

I hear Rob's voice, but the blood rushing in my ears prevents me from being able to make out the words. Grandfather comes back to my side, and I gaze up at him in supplication.

"Did he sound happy? Like he was here to enter into a lifelong loving relationship? Or determined, like he was here to break it off?"

He shakes his head. "He sounded like his usual self.

Go get a glass of water before you pass out. It's going to be fine. Who could possibly want to let go of you?"

"Many people," I say glumly, but follow his suggestion and go to the kitchen. Kethe and Fabian turn to look at me as I enter, but I say nothing, just get some water and chug it. It doesn't help—if anything, it makes things worse, sloshing around in my stomach and making me nauseous.

"Dustin?" Kethe asks. "Is Rob here?"

I nod. "Grandfather just let him through the gate." Before she asks anything else, I wander back out of the kitchen and am back in the front hall before Rob reaches the house.

Suddenly, I can't handle even a second longer of not knowing. I push past Grandfather, snatch open the front door, and bound down the steps to the driveway just as Rob drives up. He slams on the brakes to avoid hitting me with his car, then sits there, gasping, his hand pressed to his mouth.

Ooops.

I step back from the front bumper that may have brushed my leg and get into the passenger seat.

"Dustin," he gasps. "What were you *doing*? I could have killed you!"

I wave a hand. "You weren't going that fast. And we heal from almost anything. Listen, I—"

"I don't want you to have to heal from me hitting you with my car!"

"You didn't 'hit me.' Stop being dramatic. You barely touched me."

He puts the car in park and reaches for me. "Oh my god, did the car actually touch you? Where? Show me. Are you bruised? Should I call Sophie?"

"I'm fine," I declare impatiently. I can't believe he's wasting time on this when I'm *dying* to know what he's decided. "Rob, I can't wait any longer."

He blinks. "Wait for what?"

"You. To know what you want to do."

He's frowning, and my heart sinks. Maybe I should change the subject, drag him inside for lunch, and bask in his company for as long as I can.

"What I want to do about what? Are you talking about my mom's Christmas plans again? Because I already told you, it really doesn't bother me if you don't want to do everything on her itinerary. And we have ages before we have to decide, anyway."

I'm distracted by that, because I had a long chat with his mom about Christmas last week, and now I'm really excited about it. Of course, she knows the truth about Christmas, but that doesn't stop her from planning two weeks of themed activities and parties that she uses to drive fundraising. She said it's an immersive human experience for the community and that they raise more money in those two weeks than they do any other time of year. That's why she's already got the planning done, even though it's only September.

"No, we're definitely going to everything," I assert. "And we're going to watch lots of Christmas movies before then so I know what to do."

He squints at me. "That's not how... never mind. What did you mean, then?"

My purpose comes rushing back to the forefront of my mind. "Are we really going to Christmas together? Or am I going to be the sad single person trying to avoid the mistletoe so people don't feel sorry for me?" I may have already started watching Christmas movies. Research is essential.

Confusion is written all over his face, and I want to smack or kiss it away. I'm not sure which yet—it depends on whether he wants to keep me or not.

"Are you asking me if we'll still be together at Christmas?" he asks slowly. "Because I don't have a crystal ball. I hope we will be—I believe we will be—but there are no guarantees in life."

I grin so wide, it makes my cheeks ache. "So you're not ending things today?" I confirm, and he starts to laugh.

"Dustin, seriously, did you think I was? We made dinner reservations for the restaurant you want to go to next weekend!"

When he says it like that, I can see that maybe I was overreacting just a tiny bit. "I had to be sure," I protest, but there's no heat behind it. I'm too busy dragging his head close to mine so I can kiss him.

Have you ever made out in the front seat of a car? I do *not* recommend it. Aside from being ridiculously uncomfortable, with consoles and gear shifts and steering wheels bumping into you every time you move, there's just not enough space to get close. And I want to be close. I want to be pressed against Rob from shoulder to toe, want to feel the length of him against me.

Oh, and the last reason I don't recommend making out in cars?

No privacy.

"Hey! Kethe wants to know if you're going to be long. Lunch is ready." Wil bangs cheerfully on the roof of the car. He's doing it on purpose—if it were Fabian, I'd say he's really that oblivious, but Wil just likes to occasionally torment me. Maybe we can just ignore him?

"They're just kissing!" he yells, presumably to someone still inside, and Rob pulls back with a sigh.

"We'd better go in," he says, and I vow that Wil won't live another day.

Well… fine, he can live, but one day I will have my vengeance.

"Park the car first," I manage to get out through gritted teeth. "It's fine if you run over Wil's foot."

Rob laughs and puts the car in gear, but he eases his foot off the brake so slowly, there's no way he could do any harm. Wil still yelps and scrambles back like the dramatic ass he is.

I say nothing the whole time Rob is driving around the house and parking the car, and when he turns the engine off, he turns to me and grabs my hand, lifting it to his lips to kiss my palm.

A shiver runs through me. Who knew such an innocent gesture could be so arousing?

"Why don't you come and stay at my place tonight?" he suggests softly. "We'll have lots of privacy, and my bed is nice and big."

"Yes." The word comes out so fast, it's barely understandable, but from the way he smiles, he got the drift.

"Perfect."

I LOVE ROB'S HOUSE. As he says, it's bigger than what a single man really needs, but he's made it his own and uses all the space well. When I follow him inside later that afternoon, I absorb the very Rob-ness of it all and take a deep breath, feeling all my worries fall away.

Not that I have many. My biggest worries over the past few years have been my unrequited love for Rob and the fear that nobody will ever take me seriously. Here I am with Rob, about to embark upon a night of wild fucking, and even though there's some doubt about my professional integrity, people are willing to go to bat for me to run a big project. My grandfather has complete faith in me. All in all, my life is pretty good.

And it's about to get better.

As Rob drops his keys in a bowl that seems to exist just to hold keys, I wander into the little room that serves as his library-slash-study. His desk sits in the center of the room, the surface clear except for his briefcase. He's had floor-to-ceiling bookshelves built into two of the walls, and a third wall has a big bay window overlooking the walled front garden. The last wall is covered with framed postcards and photos of friends and family—Rob calls it his "life wall." A long, plush couch sits in front of it, perfect for stretching out on with a good book… or doing other things.

This is where I want Rob to fuck me the first time. This room is so special to him, and I want him to think of me every time he sets foot inside.

"Dustin?" he calls. "Do you want a drink?"

"No, thanks," I yell. I'm not thirsty, but even if I was, I wouldn't let myself get distracted.

I hear his footsteps retreating down the hall, toward the kitchen at the back of the house, and take advantage of the opportunity to get ready.

Clothes off. I hide them behind the couch, because I don't want Rob to decide he needs to fold them neatly or anything. I don't *think* he's that particular, but now is not the time to take chances.

Next, I double-check the view from the window. There's no way anyone from the street can see in without climbing the fence, and there are no buildings nearby with upper-story windows in the right—or wrong—position, but if Rob's worried, we can close the curtains. Personally, I don't care who sees me naked, and I'd love to show off my beautiful Rob too, but that's up to him to decide.

Okay… naked, check. Privacy, check. I turn toward the couch and study it. It's more than long and deep enough for us both to be comfortable. Would I be more appealing lying on it, beckoning to him? Or standing before it, beckoning to him?

Or maybe I should pretend to be coy. I could sit with a book and act all surprised when he comes in. I mean… people read naked all the time. There's nothing unusual about that, right?

The sound of Rob's footsteps approaching spur me into action. I snatch the nearest book off one of the shelves and dive for the couch, arranging myself so I'm partly reclining against one of its arms, propped on my elbow, my legs tucked casually beside me. The book is open on the couch arm, and I have just enough time to read a sentence about fungal growth—*WTF?*—before Rob appears in the doorway.

I hear him catch his breath but keep my attention on the page in front of me. I definitely picked up the wrong book, since fungal growth has been followed by discussion of putrid rot. This seems to be an old textbook of some kind rather than the novel I thought it was, and definitely isn't the sexiest subject matter.

Not that I need sexy subject matter right now. Just knowing Rob's watching me has my cock stiffening.

"What are you doing?" he asks lightly, though there's definitely a note of strain in his voice.

"Reading," I reply, not taking my eyes off the book as I turn the page. "What the *fuck*?" I leap to my feet, putting distance between me and the drawing of a maggot-laden wound. In case you were wondering, it's not less gross when it's a drawing instead of a photo.

"Papercut?" Rob inquires, coming into the room.

I shudder. "I'd take a thousand papercuts over seeing that. I'm never going to be able to close my eyes again."

Even though I'm naked, he walks past me and picks up the book from the couch.

"Ew, yes, I see what you mean," he says calmly, closing it and going to return it to its shelf. "But why were you reading a nineteenth century medical text?"

Dammit. Caught out.

"At first I thought it was a novel," I extemporize. "Because of the leather binding. I thought it was one of your original editions. And then when I realized it wasn't, I was, uh, kind of interested. Until I saw that picture."

He turns back to face me, nodding thoughtfully. "That makes perfect sense. Do you often read with no clothes on?"

"All the time," I say breezily, sitting on the couch and crossing one leg over the other knee. Then I realize that hides some of my best assets and hastily uncross, parting my legs slightly for full display. "Doesn't everyone?"

His gaze is sliding over me with such intensity, I can almost feel it. *Yessssss.* "I'd have to ask them." His reply is hoarse. "I know I don't."

"You should try it sometime. We could have a quiet evening in… reading. You and me. Snuggled up on this couch. Naked. *Reading*." I can see from his expression that he's remembering that I want to jerk myself to the sound of him reading to me, but there was so much innuendo in my tone, I doubt he thinks I actually meant reading right now.

Then he pulls himself together and grins wickedly. "What a great idea. Why not now?"

My jaw drops, but he doesn't see it, because he's turned to the bookshelves and is browsing for a book.

Browsing. For. A. Book.

While I sit here, naked!

"I'll read to you," he's saying as he runs a finger along a line of book spines. He's gone to the modern section, where none of the bindings are leather. He can't actually be serious, can he? After two weeks of torture and the promises he made me earlier today? I want to be ravished, damn him!

"Rob," I whine plaintively, and he glances over his shoulder at me.

"Yes?"

"Seriously?" I abandon all attempts at game playing. "I'm naked here, and you want to read?"

His face breaks into a grin, and he abandons the bookcases to come toward me, unbuttoning his shirt on the way. "I knew you'd cave."

I don't even care that he won our stupid little game —all that interests me is getting him naked and in me.

He joins me on the couch, still mostly clothed, and kisses me so hard, I know my lips will be swollen later. I don't care. I crawl into his lap, straddling him, then pull back with a sound of disgust. "Why do you still have clothes on?"

Chuckling, he strips off his shirt, then pushes me gently onto the couch so he can stand and get rid of his pants. That puts me almost at eye-level—mouth-level—with his beautiful cock, and I lick my lips.

Then stare curiously.

I've never actually seen a human dick before. All my sexual partners after we came to Earth were members of the community. We weren't mingling too much with humans, those first few years, and then I started college and met Rob and became celibate. Because if I couldn't have him, I wanted nobody. I'm told human cock is a lot like sorcerer cock, but I've never been with a sorcerer either. It's the same basic shape as a demon dick, although the head is more clearly defined and demons are thick from base to tip, whereas it seems that humans have a slight taper? I tilt my head to assess it better.

Rob laughs. "What are you doing?"

"Checking out your cock. I've never been with a human before."

He drops into a crouch and kisses me, closing his hand around my dick. "Mmm, I've never been with a dragon before. And I'm very curious about all these bumpy things."

We both look down at my lap as he pumps my cock, each ridge sliding through his grip. "You're like a washboard," he comments. "This is going to feel amazing when you fuck me."

A hot flush sweeps through me. "You want me to do that?" I'm vers, but the downside of being adorable is that people make assumptions.

He looks uncertain. "Unless you don't want to? I really want your ass this time, but maybe—"

"Yes! I want it. You in my ass and me in yours and each other's mouths and hands and maybe some toys? Let's do it all. Starting now." I slide a hand around the back of his neck and yank him to me.

It takes only half a second for Rob to get into it, and then he climbs up on the couch, pushing me back, lying over me while we eat each other's mouths. This is it, what I've been waiting two weeks—two years—*my whole life*—for, and it's so amazing, I could cry.

Instead, I open my legs, bend my knees, and rut against my sexy lover.

He breaks our kiss and begins working his way down my body, pausing to lick and suck and gently bite as he mutters how beautiful I am, how sexy and wonderful, how lucky he is, and I clutch his head to me. Usually I'm an active sexual partner, but something about this first time with Rob makes me want to lie back and be worshipped.

And he does. He adores every inch of me, and maybe our relationship is still new, but I swear I can feel his love. Even if he doesn't know it yet, he loves me, and it feeds something deep in my soul.

But it's not my soul that needs satisfaction right now. I whimper as Rob hovers over my cock, his hot breath washing over the sensitive skin, but he doesn't touch it. Instead, he bends his head lower and licks my balls. My whole body shudders, so he does it again.

"Like that, do you?" he murmurs. "You taste amazing."

"Please," I beg, and he chuckles.

"Please what?"

"Suck my dick! Please."

So he does. His hot, wet mouth closes around the head and slides down the shaft as he tongues over each ridge, lingering hungrily. I squeeze my eyes closed, the intensity almost too much, my hands finding their way to his hair and tangling in the short locks, urging him on.

By the time he pulls back, I'm breathing so hard I can't hear anything else, and I may have promised him all sorts of things I can't deliver. I pry my eyes open to look at his beloved face. His glasses are askew, and I release my death grip on the couch cushion to reach up and remove them. Without the lenses to hide behind, his beauty is even more apparent, but he's… different. A naughty thrill chases down my spine. Glasses-wearing Rob is my mild-mannered professor, but this Rob is my wild pirate.

"I want you in me," I whisper, and his smile is rakish, the gleam in his eyes pure lust.

But then he pulls away, and I whine. "Where are you going?"

"Lube," he replies. "We need some."

I scoff. "I can self-lube."

He freezes and blinks at me. "What? Really?"

"No. But hold out your hand, and I'll magic some lube."

Seeming dubious, he extends a hand, palm cupped, and I draw on my power and create a small puddle of lube.

"That's some party trick," he says, staring at it.

"This party is going to get boring if you don't get back to work."

He huffs a laugh, leans down to kiss me, and then

dips a finger in the lube and runs it around my hole. The combination of cold liquid and the light touch makes me jerk, and my cock, which was starting to lose interest, returns to it's hard-as-steel state.

Rob does a thorough job prepping me, one finger at a time, making sure my muscles are relaxed before he adds the next one and occasionally brushing against my prostate just to make me beg him to hurry the fuck up.

"I'm stretched," I declare. "We dragons have excellent muscle control. Fuck me already!"

Locking his gaze with mine, he leans down and gently bites my nipple at the same time his fingers peg my prostate.

I come, my back bowing as every muscle clenches in pleasure.

I didn't think I was that close, but clearly Rob knows my body better than I do—and knows how to play it like an instrument.

When I finally flop to the couch in boneless exhaustion, Rob is watching me, smirk in place.

"What are you so smug about?" I mutter, and he moves his fingers in me, making me twitch.

"You're gorgeous when you come."

"I wanted to come with you in me," I complain sulkily.

"You will," he promises. "Is there any reason you can't go again now?" He glances pointedly at my dick, which is hardening again. "I know refractory times in the community are a lot shorter than for humans, and I want to take advantage of that."

Oh, *yeah*, baby.

"If you insist." I lean up to kiss him, just because I can.

"One question," he murmurs against my lips.

"Anything. I'll do anything you want."

Pulling back, he bites my lip, then says, "I'll remember that. But what I want to ask is, do you not ejaculate when you come?"

I blink, trying to make my brain work. "Ejaculate? No. Dragons don't procreate with sex, so we don't produce semen."

"I'm going to have so many questions about that later, but for now…" He withdraws his fingers from my ass so swiftly, I gasp, then hooks my legs over his forearms, adjusts the angle of my hips, and enters me in a single hard thrust.

The air expels from my lungs in a cry of surprise and pleasure. My muscles stretch to accommodate him, and I close my eyes and give myself over to bliss as he begins to thrust, working every nerve ending, drawing almost all the way out on every thrust, forcing my body to take all of him each time. The tension in me ratchets higher and higher, tighter and tighter, until he growls, "Now, come now!" and I explode all over again as he moans and collapses over me, his cock twitching inside me.

This was worth waiting for.

CHAPTER THIRTEEN

Dustin

I WAKE up to the best morning ever.

Why is it the best morning ever? Simple. How could it be anything else when I'm in Rob's bed, snuggled up against him? When there's a pleasant soreness in my ass that I refuse to heal from having him in me three times last night? The last time, he kept telling me he wasn't young anymore, that he couldn't possibly go again.

I proved him wrong.

And yes, I am smirking smugly right now. When he wakes up, I'll have to remember to say "I told you so."

Meanwhile, I get to cuddle up to the love of my life, secure in the knowledge that we're together now, that he wants me, that I get to wake up this way as many mornings as I want to. Or as many as I can convince him to let me stay over, anyway. I'll give him a few months to get used to having me around before I move my stuff in and tell him we're living together.

As the room gradually gets lighter, I bask in all my happy feelings. I've lived a long time and have always considered myself a happy person, but this is different.

Yeah, I knew having a partner might add a new dimension to my life, that companionship and love would be a great thing to have, but this… this is far beyond what I expected. And we've only just begun.

Rob stirs behind me, pressing his lips against the back of my neck, and I shiver. "Good morning," he murmurs, his voice all growly. "How long have you been awake?"

"Not long. I'm just enjoying the first morning of the rest of our lives."

He stiffens slightly, and I wonder if maybe I'm going too fast for him. But then he relaxes and curls his body around mine.

"Are you going to class today? Want a lift to campus? Or is Fabian coming to pick you up?"

I wriggle around to face him. Our dicks rub up against each other, and mine stirs with interest. His tries to, but gives up. I guess three times is all a human can manage in one night? We'll have to work on improving his stamina.

"I'm not going to class today," I say quietly. "I might go to campus if I need to be there to drop out. But I'm no longer a college student."

He swallows hard, his gaze searching my face. "Are you sure?"

"Positive. I don't want that anymore. That part of my life is over, even if there was nothing between us." I kiss his nose. "Can I hang out here today?" *And tonight, and the rest of the week?*

"Of course," he assures me. "Make yourself at home. You know where everything is." He hesitates. "You're not going to spend the day worrying about the outreach program, are you?"

I sigh. "Maybe. A little bit." Julian should hear from Lihua at some stage today. Unless she needs more time to think about it. What if she decides she wants a week to consider? How will I cope for five more days? "But I'll try to keep busy. I need to formally drop out, and then I can keep working on alternative fundraising options. Even if we get this funding, we'll always need more."

"That's true," he agrees. "Just promise me something."

"You can have anything you want."

He smiles, and the corners of his eyes crinkle. "If you start to feel bad, or if Lihua Jiǎng decides not to fund this project, you call me. I'll leave my phone on. Don't let yourself get as upset as you were last week."

"I won't," I assure him, basking in the warmth of his care. "But turn your phone off. I like texting you during the day and I don't want to interrupt your classes. If I feel bad, I'll call someone. But just knowing you're going to come home to me will help."

He looks slightly doubtful, so I kiss him as a distraction. His cock is really trying to get in on the act when his phone blares a horrible sound. Sighing, Rob breaks our kiss.

"That's my alarm. Time to get up."

"Now?" I cry plaintively.

"Now," he says firmly, throwing back the covers. That works to my advantage, and I spread my arms to give him a clear view.

"But how can you leave me like this?"

His gaze skims down the length of me, and he clears his throat. "It's not easy. But I have to get to work."

I pout, and his control wavers. I actually see the moment when he hardens his resolve. "You can take care of it in the shower. And then when I get home, I'll be ready to go again."

That both disappoints and arouses me.

I END up going with Rob to campus. I figure it will be easier to do whatever's needed to withdraw from there than trying to do it online and over the phone. And for something that should really be quite simple, it's a lot more complicated than I expected. Turns out the university doesn't like the idea of not getting my tuition fees anymore. Even when, in a fit of exasperation, I told them they could keep what had been paid for this semester, there was a lot of humming and ahhing and a suggestion that I should speak to my adviser and maybe a counselor first. To shut them up, I went and ambushed my adviser between classes, telling her that I was dropping out and really could use her support with the administration. That led to a twenty-minute conversation over lunch, because she had no other time free today and I refused to "think it over and we'll talk later in the week." Finally, she agreed that I "have my head on straight" and sent an email supporting me.

So it's close to two o'clock before I leave the administration office with the paperwork complete. They warned me that it would take a few days to process and that any tuition due to be refunded could take longer still. I don't care. All that matters to me is that I'm no longer a student at this college, and that's one weight I can take off Rob's conscience.

I've been live-texting Rob my turmoils all day, so I send him a victory message now, as I stroll toward the cafeteria where I'm meeting Zara, and finally I get a message back.

Rob: *So glad you're happy and that it's organized. Does Fabian want to have dinner with us tonight, or are you going back with him?*

Uhh, going back? Hard no. And Fabian's not coming over either. Rob made me promises this morning that don't need a third wheel.

Me: *Fabian has to get back early, so it's just you and me for dinner. And afters.*

I briefly consider going to see him in his office—I know he's done with classes for the day—but decide it's safer if I don't. We should get a little distance between student-me and boyfriend-me before I start visiting him at work. Especially since his office is in the same hallway as so many of my other professors.

Rob: *LOL fine, you minx. Just you and me and "afters." I'm leaving at quarter after five. If you're still around, I'll give you a ride.*

Me: *Why Professor, I didn't know you offered those services. Ride you? I'd love to.*

Smiling smugly at the thought of his face when he reads that, I walk into the cafeteria and look around for Zara. It's late enough that there are heaps of available tables, but she's not sitting at any of them.

"There you are," she says from behind me, and I turn around. Her grin is wide. "How'd it go yesterday? I can't believe you didn't text to let me know. But I guess it's good news, because you don't look miserable."

I grin back. "It's good news," I confirm, and she lets out a very un-Zara-like squeal. "Food first," I demand, because wrangling with bureaucrats is hungry work. But soon we're sitting at a table by the window and she's staring at me expectantly.

"He laughed at me for being nervous and said he just assumed I'd know that he wanted to be with me," I paraphrase, not mentioning our plans for the weekend. Zara would call me an idiot, and I've had enough of that from her.

She puts a hand over her heart. "Awww. But I knew that would happen. He's been totally into you for the past two weeks. No way was he changing his mind at the last minute." She looks around, then leans closer. "Did you do it?"

"Do what?" I know what.

"Have sex," she hisses. I say nothing, and her face falls. "No? Why? Was it because you were at your grandfather's place?" She leans back and folds her arms. "I was so sure you were going to spend the rest of the day having dirty sex with him."

I shake my head. "Well, we didn't." I pause just long enough for her disappointment to settle in. "We spent all night doing that."

Her head snaps up. "What? Shut *up*! Was it amazing?"

I nod, grinning so wide, my face hurts. "It really, really was. He's perfect, Zara. In every way. I spent the night at his place and came in with him this morning. Which reminds me…" I snatch up the folder with all my unenrollment forms. "I am no longer a student at this college."

Her reaction this time is mixed. "I know that's what you wanted, but I'm going to miss seeing you every day," she confesses.

The realization that I'm no longer going to be able

to gossip with her when we're supposed to be paying attention in class, or snatch a coffee break between study groups, hits me hard.

"I'll miss you too. But I'll be much closer now, since Rob lives only ten minutes from campus. I can still come in and have lunch with you sometimes, and we can catch up in the evenings since I don't need to drive all the way home anymore. Well, the evenings when I'm not busy doing Rob."

She coughs. "Thanks for that visual."

"Oh, that was nothing. Let me tell you about how he—"

"Thanks, Dustin." She holds up a hand. "I'm really fine with it. I'll probably have him next year for my creative writing classes, and I think being his student will be easier if I don't know anything intimate about him."

"Probably," I agree. "I certainly couldn't sit still in his class now that I know what it's like to be under him."

"Another visual I really didn't need. Thanks so much."

"If you think you didn't need it, you visualized him wrong." I smile, remembering Rob's beautiful naked body and especially his thick dick. I wonder if I can get him to pose for pictures? He's surprisingly shy about his body, muttering about going soft in middle age, but I'd really enjoy a nude poster of him.

My phone rings before she can reply. A quick glance shows Julian's name on the screen, and my palms start to sweat.

"Are you going to answer that?" Zara asks.

"I'm afraid to. My whole future is on the line."

She forks up some more salad. "You're such a drama queen."

Steeling myself, I snatch up the phone and answer it.

"Hello?" I'm so proud that there's only the faintest tremor in my voice.

"We got it, Dustin."

I sag in my chair and brace my forearm on the table to avoid sliding to the floor. I didn't realize exactly how worried I was until this moment.

Julian's still talking, but the rush of relief drowned him out.

"Sorry, Julian, I missed that. Can you say it again, please?"

"Of course. Lihua apologized for the confusion and for the insult to you. She said she spoke to her lawyer about the source of his information and was disappointed by the lack of concrete evidence. He's been told to do better or find another job. She wanted me to tell you that she's thrilled to find her instincts were, in fact, right about you and that she's excited for you to get started right away. She also thinks she may be able to interest some acquaintances in donating to an expanded program, so you might want to get moving on those plans."

Joy explodes in me, my magic racing through my veins. There's the sound of yelling from outside, and Zara and I both look out the window... at the trees bursting into full spring bloom right before our eyes.

In September.

Oops.

There's a group of people staring at those trees... and at the garden beds where out-of-season tulips and daffodils are springing up in twos and threes, bright and cheerful and not supposed to be there.

"What the hell?" Zara asks, leaning closer to the window. "They weren't like that when I came in!"

"Uh, yeah, me either. What the hell," I echo. "Um, Julian, thank you so much—this is incredible news. What's the next step?" I put a tight rein on my magic. I am in so much trouble.

"Can you come to my office tomorrow? I'll introduce you to the team and we can kick things off."

"Sounds great." My attention is now mostly on the growing group outside. Fuck. Fuck. I need to call Grandfather. Or Percy. He'll know what to do. It would be really bad if I just accidentally outed the community to humans because I was so happy I lost control like a fledgling.

I manage to end my call with Julian, then say to Zara, "Bathroom!" She barely notices me leaving, she's so engrossed in the "miracle" that's taken place outside.

Huddling in one of the stalls in the otherwise thankfully empty bathroom, I call Percy.

"Dustin? Hi. What's up?"

"I fucked up," I whisper. "Please help me!" I quickly tell him what's happened.

"Okay," he says after a short pause. "Is there any evidence, even anecdotal, that you were connected to this? Did you point toward the garden before it happened or anything like that?"

"No. This is sometimes a side effect of dragon magic," I explain. "If it gets away from us, it tries to help things… be stronger? There were probably some healed papercuts and sniffles in the cafeteria too. But I didn't direct it. It just got out and did its own thing."

To my relief, he laughs. "You're fine, then. I'll call CSG and have them keep an eye on the situation in case any questions start getting close, but if there's no way to connect you to this, people are going to marvel over it for a few days and then forget. You'd be amazed at the mental acrobatics humans put themselves through to explain things. Believe me, nobody is even going to consider magic."

I breathe a little easier. "Are you sure?"

"Positive," he assures me. "So you got your funding? Congratulations!"

My happiness is lacking the exuberance of before. "Thanks, but I can't help wondering if maybe the lawyer was right. I mean, look what I just did."

"Dustin," Percy says firmly, "we all get a bit carried away sometimes. We all make mistakes, even the most responsible of us. You immediately took steps to fix things and asked for help, which is exactly what a responsible person does. Stop doubting yourself—we don't."

A stall in the men's room outside the cafeteria is probably not the best place for an epiphany, but it strikes me all the same. Yesterday, Grandfather said he wanted me to get involved with his government. Julian is willing to associate me with the reputation of his charity. Lihua Jiǎng is happily giving me piles of money.

And Rob compromised his morals for me.

None of them doubt me. It's time for me to live up to their expectations.

"Thanks, Percy. I'll be in the city tomorrow—can I have lunch with you and Grandfather?"

"We'd love that. Now go pretend to be amazed by these late-blooming flowers. Or is it early?"

"I'll let you know what story people come up with. I

hope it's something wild." And as far from the truth as possible.

CHAPTER FOURTEEN

Rob

It takes only five days of being with Dustin to know my life will never be the same.

And I'm okay with that. In fact… I love it. I love waking up with him wrapped around me. I love the way he's happy to wake up if it means sex or cuddles, but whines if it means actually getting up. I love the enthusiasm he has for everything, for how focused and determined he is about his youth programs. I love that he makes coming home a joy. I love that he's obsessed with reality TV and cheesy soap operas and makes me sit with him to watch. He doesn't care if I'm reading or grading papers, just as long as I'm there with him. And I love that he loves me, every inch of me. It's hard to be unhappy when someone wants you so completely.

And today I get to learn a bit more about him.

We drove out to Here Be Dragons last night to spend the weekend. Dustin explained that if he doesn't shift back to his dragon form semiregularly, he starts to feel off-kilter, but because of his size as a dragon, it's not something he can just do here in town. I'm not prepared to be apart from him for the whole weekend so soon, so I was thrilled when he invited me to stay. Plus, I like Dustin's family, zany as they are, and the estate is beautiful. It's no hardship to spend a weekend in the country.

Friday night dinner was a loud and raucous affair, with everyone talking at once, trying to catch each other up on the events of the week. As best I could tell, Fabian had a three-way that was a crushing disappointment; Sophie has begun testing slug slime for… something, I zoned out when she began describing how it tasted; and Steffen was kicked out of a department store for telling patrons they were being watched. The whole time, Brandt beamed indulgently from his seat at the head of the table.

Then after dinner, Dustin whisked me up to his room, set a privacy ward, and told me it was time to make two years' of fantasies come true.

So this morning I'm happily tired, a little sore, and in awe of his imagination. I'm sacked out on the terrace, coffee in hand, talking about nothing in particular with Percy while the rest of the household strolls down to the bottom of the lawn.

To the launch/land zone.

I'm going to get to watch Dustin shift.

"How does this work, exactly?" I ask Percy. "Is there any chance of people seeing them?"

"No," he assures me. "They'll use distortion shields to hide from human eyes. All eyes, actually, except for other dragons and anyone they choose to make an exception to the shield. Which is usually just me, but will also be you now."

"And they'll just… change? Is it painful?" I could have asked Dustin about this, but I didn't want to inadvertently say something offensive. And anyway, he distracted me. A lot.

"Not at all. Dragon magic is unique. They just redirect their energy and change forms. Just be warned, they're *big*."

I gaze across the vast expanse of lawn. "How big?"

He smiles. "Well, we're sitting up here so we don't accidentally get in the way while they change."

Wow. I swallow. "That big, huh?"

His chuckle is warm. "Don't worry, they're very self-aware and graceful. Once they've changed, we'll go down so you can see up close and Dustin can nuzzle you. They're very big on nuzzling. Then we'll enjoy the sunshine while they stretch their wings a bit." He shoots me a sly sideways glance. "Before you know it, you'll be going up with Dustin."

"Sure," I say, because "no way in hell" seems rude. Besides, it's not that I'm against flying on dragonback. Part of me is thrilled by the idea. I just need time to get my head around the logistics first.

Down at the bottom of the lawn, the action begins.

Brandt shifts first, and I gasp. Percy was right about how big dragons are, but it's not just that. There's this incredible presence in this form… that extra layer of *something* that you can see in their eyes when they're biped makes so much sense now. And Brandt is gorgeous. His scales are iridescent, shifting between blue and purple in the morning light.

The others quickly shift as well, shades of red and green and pink and glittering yellow-gold. The golden dragon is Kethe, and Percy explains that dragons are born with very pale coloring that deepens over time. Once a dragon reaches a certain age, their scales attain added perspective, making them iridescent or glittery or reflective.

Dustin is a stunning sky blue, and I can't take my eyes off him. Like the others, he's big, and there's not a lot of room left on the lawn.

"Come on," Percy says, and I don't need to be told twice, hurrying down the steps from the terrace and weaving among dragon limbs until I reach Dustin.

He lowers his head, and I catch my breath when I see that his eyes are the same in this form. Bigger, but the same color and with the same sparkle.

Then he nuzzles me, and since his head is bigger than my entire body, I lurch back and windmill my arms in an attempt to stay standing. "Hey, gentle!"

He pouts.

I know that sounds ridiculous—giant dragon, pouting—but I swear he does, and he's so completely my Dustin that I can't help laughing. I lay my hands on his cheek, and the scales don't feel like I expected. Although I'm not sure what I expected—hard? Slimy? Sharp? Instead, they're as soft as the finest leather, and I stroke.

Dustin nuzzles me once more, gently this time, then nudges me back toward the terrace. I go reluctantly, glancing back over my shoulder a few times.

Percy joins me, and we watch as, one at a time, they launch into the sky.

"You're sure nobody else can see them?" I ask anxiously. I don't want Dustin in any danger.

"Positive," he assures me. "They're completely shielded from casual onlookers."

We sit back down and chat, our eyes on the sky where our respective boyfriends are playing. And yes, playing is the right word. I'm not sure exactly what the game is, but it seems to be a cousin of tag. After a while, they get bored with that and start flying way up into the sky, until they're barely visible to the naked eye, then diving back down at frightening speeds, only to pull up before they crash into the trees.

"I can't watch this," I confess, but I don't look away. If Dustin crashes, I want to be there as soon as possible.

"I don't love these stunts either," Percy admits. "But they're very experienced. They've all been doing this for a long time."

It's possible they heard us, because shortly after that, they switch games again, now indulging in aerobatics that make me dizzy to watch. They're having fun, though, so I sit back and relax and enjoy the sunshine and Percy's company while Dustin and Sophie spiral around each other at breakneck speeds.

Eventually, they tire of that too and head off for a long flight.

"Come on," Percy says, standing. "We'll get lunch ready for when they get back. They'll be hungry."

DUSTIN and I spend Saturday afternoon hanging out with his family, then we all watch *John Wick* after dinner. For reasons I don't understand, Fabian keeps asking when John Smith will appear.

"There's no John Smith, Fabian," Kethe says wearily. "It's been two years. Why can't you remember that?"

I decide not to ask.

After, Dustin and I go up to his room and cuddle in

the armchair, sitting in the dark and admiring the starlit sky through the window. I can't help remembering what he said that night at my parents' party, about how the stars are different here and that for a long time, he couldn't even see the stars on his homeworld.

I hope he's enjoying them now.

"Was it okay?" he asks suddenly. "Today, I mean. When I shifted."

I kiss the top of his head, and a bright bit of color flutters down to rest on the chair arm. A kiss to add to his hoard. It makes me smile.

"You were beautiful. I've never seen anything as gorgeous as you in your dragon form. Except maybe you in your biped form."

"Sweet talker."

"I mean it, though. You're amazing, no matter which form you're in. And I was very impressed by your flying skills."

"I was showing off a bit," he admits. "I wanted you to see what I can do." He wriggles around and tips his head back to look at me. "Would you maybe want to come flying with me one day? No fancy stuff, I swear. But it's something I want to share with you."

"I would, definitely. How would it work, exactly? Is there somewhere for me to hold on? Or would you carry me in your... uh, hands? Claws?"

He shakes his head. "No, I wouldn't carry you. We use harnesses for people to ride us, so there's no chance of you getting jostled off or your hands getting tired or anything. It's really simple. Percy goes up with Grandfather all the time—that's usually how they get to and from the city."

"That sounds safe enough. Is it comfortable for you? I don't want to hurt you or anything."

"Pfft. As if you could, puny little human like you."

I tickle him, and he squirms and giggles.

"Okay, okay, I surrender! You're a big, bad, dangerous human!"

"You surrendered awfully fast," I note, kissing his neck. "Could it be that you're super ticklish?"

"So when do you think you'll want to come flying with me?" he asks hastily, and I grin.

"Soon. In the meantime, let's talk more about how ticklish you are."

CHAPTER FIFTEEN

Rob

ONE MONTH LATER

SOMETIMES WHEN I'M lying awake in bed with Dustin snuggled up beside me, looking like an angel as he sleeps peacefully—which, believe me, is *far* from true—I want to kick myself for those two weeks I made us wait. I don't think that time was wasted—we got to know each other so much better, and I don't regret a second of it. But I do wish we could have spent some more of it in bed together. In fact, I wish I'd thrown all my scruples to the wind the second I saw him in that first class, two years ago. We could have had two extra years together.

I'm so very conscious of the fact that I'm middle-aged. Dustin may be far, far older than me, but I'm only human, and I'm halfway—possibly more—through my life already. The forty or so years we'll have together will ultimately just be the blink of an eye in Dustin's life. And even though we've only been together six weeks—including the sexless first two—I already resent every second I was without him.

How does my mom get through the day knowing she's going to get older and older and die while Julian still has decades—centuries—remaining? It's not that bad now—as I understand it, Mom's finally reached the human equivalent of Julian's age. For the first time since they met, they don't look like a May-October couple. But within the next ten years, Mom's going to move into the next stage of her life, and Julian won't.

The urge to talk to her about it is so strong, I find myself slipping out of bed, leaving Dustin to whine before he latches onto my pillow and buries his face in it. A quick pause to admire the smooth line of his back and the way his blond hair curls around his nape, and then I yank on pajama pants and slip out of the room.

Downstairs, I get the coffee started and ignore my healthy cereal in favor of dunking Ritz crackers into the jar of Nutella Dustin bought. Don't knock it until you've tried it—the combo of salty and sweet, crunchy and creamy, is perfect. I don't normally keep Nutella in the house, but Dustin was watching porn and saw something he wanted to try, so…

And don't worry—this isn't the jar we used for that. The grocery store was having a sale, and it turns out my flirtatious darling is tight with cash and never passes up a twofer sale.

Grabbing my coffee and phone, I abandon the crackers and Nutella and head for the library. It's always been my favorite room in the house, but Dustin's fondness for feeling me up in there makes it even more attractive to me now, and I curl up on the couch and dial Mom. She's always been an early riser; that's where I get it from.

"Good morning, my favorite son," she says warmly after one ring.

"Good morning, my favorite mom," I reply, smiling. "I didn't wake you, did I?"

She scoffs. "Please. I've already showered and gotten a load of laundry on. Julian's still dozing, though."

"So's Dustin. But you're a bit ahead of me; I've only managed coffee so far." I frown. "Doesn't Liana do your laundry?" The housekeeper they had when I was growing up retired years ago, but I've met Liana, and I can't imagine her being pleased that Mom's upsetting her system.

"Liana and I have come to an agreement. Since I like to potter around in the mornings before she gets here, she leaves me a list every week of things I'm allowed to do. She presorted the laundry and even measured out the detergent so I wouldn't mess it up." There's a thread of amusement in Mom's voice, since she's never messed up laundry before. "One day, I'm hoping she'll let me unload the dishwasher, but she's convinced I'll put everything back in the wrong places."

I laugh. "You adore her, don't you?"

"I really, really do. But you didn't call me at six in the morning to talk about Liana."

"No." I sigh. "I'm not sure why I called, really."

"Liar."

"Mom!"

"Oh, please. I've known you your whole life. I spent twenty-six hours in labor pushing you out of me. I can tell when you're lying."

"Thanks for the visual," I murmur automatically, though she's said it so many times it's pretty much lost impact. "It's not a big lie. I'm really not sure why I called. It's not like there's anything you can do."

"You don't know that," she protests. "I'm Super-mom, thank you very much."

I grin, remembering when I used to call her that. "I know." Still, I hesitate. It seemed like a good idea to call her before, but now… it's just cruel to remind her how little time she and Julian have left together. And that he'll continue on after she's gone, alone without her.

"Robert," she warns. "Don't make me count to three."

The chuckle bursts from me. "Okay, okay. I was just… thinking about how I'm already halfway through my life, but Dustin has a long time left. And that in the greater scheme of his life, our time together will just be a short interlude. And that got me thinking about you and Julian and how very soon, things are going to change for you." There. That's the nicest way I can think of to say it.

But I guess it still hits a sore spot, because Mom's silent.

"Mom? I'm sorry. I should never have brought it up. I—"

"Hush, please, Rob. I'm trying to think," she says absently. "Crap. I guess I should have had this talk with you after all. But we just thought it might be better to wait."

I suddenly feel like a teenager again. "What talk? Wait for what?" A horrible, ridiculous thought pops into my head. "You're not about to tell me that you and Julian have some kind of suicide pact, are you?" I can't fathom that Mom would allow Julian to do that after all the work they've both done raising awareness and money for mental health and suicide prevention.

"Of course not," she snaps, which is a relief. Selfish as it is, I've been comforted by the thought that when I eventually lose my mom, I'll still have my stepdad. "Just let me tell this in my own time. It's complicated." She hesitates. "Maybe we should do this face-to-face."

"Mom!" If she thinks I'm going to wait to hear what she's planning to tell me, she has another think coming.

Her sigh is hefty enough to be called a gust of wind. "Okay, fine. Are you sitting down?"

Oh my god, what is she about to tell me?

"Sitting down," I confirm, leaning over to put my still half-full coffee mug on the floor. I don't want to accidentally spill the hot liquid on myself if what she's about to say is actually that shocking.

"Since the dragons and elves came to Earth, we've learned some new stuff. Well, it was actually old stuff that we'd forgotten about. Not *we* we, but we as a general society."

"Mom!" I'm going to strangle her.

"I'm sorry, Rob, I know I'm making a mess of this, but bear with me. I have to lay the groundwork."

Knowing my mom, that means I'm in for an hour-long meandering story that only has a little bit to do with the point.

"Do you have to? Just give me the bottom line."

"Well…" She hesitates.

"Bottom line, Mom."

"I can extend my life to be as long as Julian's," she blurts.

My head spins, and all I can think is how glad I am that I put the mug down.

"Rob?"

I suck in a breath and hear it rasp in my too-tight throat.

"Rob?" Now she sounds worried.

"I'm here," I manage. "Uh… maybe a little more groundwork would be good." I need the time to get my head around this. Did she really say she could extend her life?

And does that mean I can too?

Hope is a desperate creature clawing inside me. To have more time with Dustin… I reach with shaking hands for my coffee, needing the hot liquid to ground me.

"It's a long and complicated story," Mom's saying. "The gist is that humans are able to perform magic too —we forgot we had the ability after the species wars, along with forgetting all the other species existed. But all the other species forgot we could do that too. I'm not entirely clear on how it came up again—it was around the time of the migration, so it could be that the dragons and elves just reminded everybody, but I've heard a few things that make me think someone here had already rediscovered it. Anyway, the long and short of it is, even though it's different to what the elves do, some of the principles are the same, and one of those is that it can be used to extend a human lifespan."

I've never felt this stupid before in my life, not even the time I was dating a physicist and he would talk about his work while my hates-math brain struggled to make sense of what he was saying. For some reason, this is even harder. My mind is desperately trying to absorb what Mom is telling me.

"H-How?" I ask. I have so many other questions—

"why" is another biggie—but that's the one that comes out.

"It's complicated," Mom says again, and I've never hated any phrase as much as that one right now. "There's a whole lot of meditation to start with. I was only really interested in the life-expansion part of it, but there's the potential to learn to do all sorts of things."

I drag the shattered pieces of my intelligence together and force myself to think. "Is this common knowledge?"

"No. Not even in the community. There would be too much risk that it would get out among the general human populace, and even if it didn't, there are a lot of people in the community who wouldn't react well to knowing that humans can use magic. For now, it's been quietly circulated to those of us who are in mixed-species relationships, particularly if we're older and have less time to learn what needs to be learned. I think CSG wants to ease in, see how things go before expanding it to every human who knows about the community."

"That makes sense," I mutter. "So Dustin would know about this?"

"I don't know, sweetheart. You'd have to ask him."

I swallow the lump in my throat and ask, "You're not going to get any older?" Is that what she's telling me?

She hesitates again, and there's a rasp in her voice when she says, "No, Rob. I'm not going to get any older."

Tears run down my face, and I pinch the bridge of my nose, nostrils flaring as I suck in air. I've lived my whole life knowing that at some stage, I'd lose Mom… my only parent, the only person I could rely on for my first seven years, the one person who has always been unconditionally there for me. But that's normal, right? Parents getting older and dying… that's something everyone on Earth has to deal with. I didn't realize how relieved I would be to know I can have longer with my mom.

She's still talking. "Well, I *am* going to get older, but it'll be more controlled. I'm going to pace my life to Julian's. And—" Her voice breaks. "And now that you're with Dustin…"

I swipe the tears from my cheeks, understanding her meaning without the words needing to be said. "I guess I need to talk to Dustin." Has he not mentioned this because he doesn't know? Because it slipped his mind? Because he thought it might be too early in our relationship? Because he's worried about what my reaction will be?

Because he doesn't want to spend forever with me?

I push that last, insidious question aside. Whatever reason Dustin hasn't brought this up yet, I know it's not that. We might still be new, but I don't doubt his commitment to me… and anyway, extending my own life with the use of magic (oh my god, it's surreal) doesn't mean we'll be tied together until we die.

Does it? Do dragons die if they're not killed? Do I even want to live indefinitely? I mean… that's a long time. I'd see a lot of things change that maybe I wouldn't want to. Dustin had to watch his world cease to exist—is that the kind of thing I want to face?

I need to learn more about this.

"You should," Mom agrees. "It's a tricky subject to bring up. Julian and I wondered when to discuss it with you and his kids. We figured you'd notice eventually."

A sound breaks from my throat that might have been

a laugh if I wasn't feeling so emotional. "It might have taken us a while, but we'd have seen it in the end," I agree.

"Seen what in the end?" a new voice asks, and I snap my head around toward where Dustin's lounging naked in the doorway. The second he sees my face, the flirty smile disappears and he strides into the room. "Who upset you?" he demands. "What's wrong?" He crawls onto the couch beside me and wraps his arms and legs around me, cocooning me in the safety of his embrace.

Then he snatches the phone from me.

"Hey!"

"Who is this?" he barks. "What did you say to upset Rob?"

"It's my mom," I tell him, but he's listening intently to whatever she's saying.

"Okay," he says finally. "We'll call you later." Then he ends the call.

"Um, excuse me? What if I wanted to say goodbye?"

"We'll talk to her later. She said it was important for you and me to talk first." He drops my phone to the floor, then takes my now empty mug and drops that too. Thank fuck for plush rugs. "What's upset you? Tell me, and I'll fix it."

I could never love anyone more than I do him. I snuggle into his embrace and lay my head against his. "It's fine," I murmur, kissing his hair. "I was a bit antsy this morning, thinking about how we won't have that much time together before I get old and die, and Mom told me something that was a bit of a shock."

He pulls back and frowns at me. "Why didn't you wake me? You should always wake me if you're upset."

My smile comes unbidden. "You were sleeping so peacefully. I wasn't going to wake you for something you could do nothing about."

"Doesn't matter." He shakes his head. "Wake me anyway. Nothing's ever so bad when you've got someone to share it with. What did your mom tell you that was a shock?"

There's a note in his voice on that last sentence that makes me think he knows. I pinch him—not hard.

"Ow!" He pouts at me. "What was that for?"

"Because you already know exactly what Mom told me," I say sternly—then ruin it by bending my head to kiss where I pinched. I can't resist that pout, so I kiss it too.

"Not *exactly* what she said," he informs me breathlessly when the kiss eventually ends. "I only suspected based on the subject matter."

"Is there a reason you never mentioned the subject to me earlier?"

His eyes widen, and he gazes at me guilelessly. "I thought you knew. Your mom is married to an incubus, and I'd heard a few years back at CSG that they were going to tell all the older mixed-species couples… so I just assumed you knew." He frowns. "Wait, does this mean you don't know?"

"I *didn't* know until Mom just told me. She and Julian hadn't worked out how they wanted to bring it up, so they just put it off." Seeing his frown deepen, I check to make sure we're not talking at cross purposes. "The subject is humans being able to use magic to extend their lives, right?"

He nods, but the frown is still there. "So nobody has talked to you about it? Learning to use magic, I mean? You haven't already frozen the aging process?"

Oh. *Oh.* That frown is because he's concerned about the exact same thing that was worrying me before. I kiss him again, utterly delighted that I'm going to be able to do so for many, many more years longer than I'd thought, but he breaks away.

"Rob," he whines, "this is important."

"I know. And no, I have no idea how to use magic. Can you teach me?" A tingle of excitement runs through me. Aside from the obvious joy of extending my life and having more time with him, there's also the huge thrill of being able to use magic. Since the day I found out other species existed, I've had a tiny niggle of envy for all the amazing abilities they have. I pushed it aside and considered myself lucky to be part of their world, even on the fringes, but now…

I'm going to learn magic.

Dustin's lips are pursed. "I don't think I can," he says, shaking his head. "Maybe one of the elves could, but dragon magic is so different from what even they do. It might be best to go to the source for this."

"What source?" And there go my naughty daydreams of us having naked "tutoring" sessions. I was halfway through planning the reward system, too.

"Noah."

Dragging my attention away from thoughts of blowjobs for each successful attempt at magic use, I focus fully on him. "Who's Noah?" A vague memory rises from the back of my mind. "Do you mean the admin for the lucifer's team?" There was a lot of discussion when Sam Tiller became lucifer and picked a human to be the administrator for his senior team. Even I heard about it, and I wasn't paying that much attention.

"Yep. We're friends. Well…" He screws his nose up. "…friendly acquaintances. He doesn't want to kill me as much as most people. I think." There's a brief pause while he appears to ponder whether this Noah person actually wants to kill him. "Anyway, he's the one who rediscovered that humans can use magic, and I've seen him do some pretty advanced things. I think he'd be a good person for you to talk to."

"I don't know that we need to pull strings. I'm sure whatever teaching program CSG has set up will be fine," I begin. Noah is probably busy, what with having a senior-ish government job, and if he really does want to kill Dustin, I'm not keen to spend a lot of time with him.

But Dustin's jaw has set stubbornly, the same way it did when I told him we couldn't be together, and we all know how that turned out. So I sigh. "But if you think Noah is the best option, I'm happy to defer to your expertise."

A smile blooms on his face. "Thank you. Just talk to him, even if he doesn't end up being your teacher. I'll call him later." The smile changes from sunny pleasure to sultry seduction. "I don't like waking up without you."

I lean in and kiss him. I'll never get tired of being able to do that. "I don't either. But you were so peaceful… and quiet."

He huffs. "I'm going to pretend you didn't say that, because I don't want to get into a discussion about how demure and quiet I always am." My laugh cuts him off, and he glares. "That's it. Get naked, then on your knees, facing the back of the couch."

I hide my smile as I obey, bracing my forearms along the high back of the couch and tilting my hips to pop my ass out. I love bossy Dustin. This is going to be fun.

"Because you were so mean, there will be minimal foreplay," he declares, then runs a hand down my spine, traces a finger along my crack, and takes hold of my balls. I shiver as he rolls them, my cock getting hard faster than I would've thought possible before I met him.

Then he bites my ass.

"Ow!" I yelp.

"I needed a taste." He slaps where he bit, sharpening the fading stab of pain. "You have such a biteable tushie."

"Ah, thanks?" Secretly, I preen. I'm in my midforties, and my ass is definitely not as perky as his, no matter how hard I try to stay in shape. It's nice to know my body pleases him.

He presses his whole body up against my back, his cock nestling in my crack, and kisses the back of my neck. "Ready?" he murmurs.

"Hurry up. You're all talk and no action."

The sound he makes is pure pique. Teasing him is so much fun. And despite the way he's muttering about me being rude, he's incredibly gentle when his lube-wet fingers begin to stretch me. I relax and put my head down on my arms, enjoying the feeling of him fingering me. My hole has always been really sensitive, and it's not long before my dick is twitching with every movement he makes.

"Dustin, I'm ready," I hiss, shifting slightly to increase the friction on my cock. I'm going to need to have this couch professionally cleaned, with the amount of time Dustin and I spend fucking on it.

"You're ready when I say you're ready," the little shit insists, but a minute later, he withdraws his fingers and I feel the head of his cock catch against my rim. Then he's pushing in, slowly, stretching me, and the burn is so delicious. Each of the ridges on his dick feels like being breached anew, and when he's all the way inside, they rub against my nerve endings like nothing else can.

He fucks me slowly, deliberately, taking care *not* to hit my prostate, working me up into a frenzy before he finally reaches around me and grips my cock. A whimper catches in my throat.

"Wanna come?" he whispers.

"Please." It's a broken gasp.

He pumps me once, twice, three times, and I break apart, spurting, my ass clenching around him. In the next moment he cries out also, then curls around me, holding me tight.

And I get to spend the rest of eternity with him.

CHAPTER SIXTEEN

Dustin

"...AND that's what I want to focus the schedule on for the first month," I finish. "I think it's important to assess what everyone really needs before we go ahead and start locking activity plans in place." I look around the board-room, relieved to see nods and small smiles on most of the faces. The board of directors appointed to oversee my youth program is drawn from other charitable boards within the community. Julian assured me they were all enthusiastic about the program and looking forward to seeing what I could do with it, and Lihua Jiǎng, who was appointed due to the magnificent amount of money she gave us, backed him up on that. But just because people are excited about a project doesn't mean they're going to agree with my way of doing it.

"That sounds good, Your Highness," Matilda, a felid shifter with a background in health services, begins. I try not to wince at the ridiculous title. Julian and Lihua have both told me that I need to take advantage of it and the benefits it can give me. For some absurd reason, some people think an accident of birth has bearing on my fitness to do this job. I think it's ridiculous, but I'm also willing to use everything at my disposal to get this program running, including my connection to Grandfather, so…

"Just to be clear, though, you do have a planned activity schedule prepared?"

I force a smile and make a mental note to have words with Julian later. I've read up on Matilda's background—and everyone else's—and she's certainly qualified to be on this board, but clearly she didn't do her homework. "Yes, of course. There are several initial options in the business plan. Each one targets a specific area I believe may be identified as our primary area of need, but they're designed so we can tweak them easily to fit our overall needs. I don't want to focus too much on, say, teaching kids to interact with humans and ignore other equally important areas. We'll be able to assess what the priorities are during that first month and adjust and implement our plans quickly."

She nods, paging through the thick bound document in front of her—which she obviously didn't read before this meeting. "Okay, I see them now. Yes, these look good. I like that you've allowed for physical and mental health clinics in all the options."

"That's not negotiable," I agree. "In regional and rural areas, there's often a lack of access to health services, and that can lead to lack of motivation to keep on top of health. One of our priorities is to teach these kids to think of their health as something they need to maintain with regular checkups when they're feeling well and immediate attention when something's wrong. We need to support that by giving them access to those services." The college town we're starting in has a decent range of medical services for humans, and a less-decent-but-still-adequate range for the community, but I want specialist youth services. And I want them so deeply entrenched in the program that when the time comes to expand to other locations, nobody will whine about the cost of including health services in remote areas.

"And you plan to open in January?" Julian asks with a twinkle in his eye.

"We're actually hoping for mid-December," I announce, and a murmur runs around the table. "The initial proposal planned for January, but things have been going our way and we're a bit ahead of schedule. I'm excited about the opportunity to leverage the human holiday season as a relaxed introduction to the program. We think interspersing craft activities and singing and learning human folklore and history in among our needs assessments will help the kids get used to each other and the program and enable them to settle more easily when we introduce the permanent schedule."

"I like it," Lihua declares. "Humans may base most of their holiday traditions on their made-up religions, but that doesn't mean they're not interesting and some-times fun."

I smile and incline my head in thanks.

She looks around the table. "Do we have any other questions for Prince Dustin?"

There's a chorus of nos and a few heads being

shaken, so she wraps up the meeting and dismisses everyone. I expect them to leave immediately—most of them are busy and important people—but surprisingly, a fair few stick around to chat… with me. They ask me questions about the program, ask my opinions on wider issues, and one mentions an opening coming up on another charity board and suggests I express interest.

My first instinct is to decline—after all, I have no experience with sitting on a charitable board—but instead I thank him and write down the details. Why shouldn't I take a shot? This is what I want to do, right? Help people? This is what I *am* doing with the current outreach program. I have skills and knowledge that are applicable to this sort of thing. Maybe I hadn't planned to split my focus quite this soon, but there's no harm in checking it out. And I can't deny how amazing it feels to have him suggest it. Amazing and humbling and validating in a way I used to despair of ever feeling. People have enough faith in my abilities—in me—that they want to give me more responsibility.

Fuck yeah!

The room slowly empties out, until it's just me and Julian. He leans against the boardroom table and grins at me. "How are you feeling?"

I take a second to think about it. "Great," I admit. "I was worried about this meeting—"

"I could tell."

"—but I feel better now." I shoot him a curious look. "How could you tell?"

He laughs. "Dustin, I may not know you that well, but you had the same look on your face when you came in here today that you had when you were chasing Rob at my place that night."

"Oh." I laugh too. "Yeah, the feeling was almost the same. Not as bad this time, though." Satisfaction rises in me like a wave. I'm killing it with getting what I want lately. First Rob, now the outreach program.

"Speaking of my stepson, how's he doing? With, uh…" He glances at the door, which is still open. "With his new hobby?"

It's not hard to guess he's talking about Rob's attempts to master wielding magic. I look at the door too and pick my words very carefully. "I think pretty well. He's frustrated by all the, uh, prep work that's needed, but his instructor says he's doing fine."

I called Noah Cage the same day Rob found out about human magic use. I'm not as good friends with him as I am with some of the others on the team, but when I told him I was in love with a human who already knew all about us, I didn't even have to ask for his help.

"Bring him to see me," he said before I even finished talking. "I can teach him what he needs to know and answer his questions."

It reminded me once again of how it felt when Percy invited us all to live on Earth, no questions asked, no conditions, and saved us from extinction. Even if Grandfather wasn't madly in love with him, even if he wasn't a great person who's always stepped up when I needed help, I'd do anything for Percy just because of that.

Julian's nodding. "Great, that's great. It was a big relief to Erika to be able to tell him. And to know that he'd—er, that he was going to take up the same hobby." He winces. Keeping a secret within his own office, among his people, seems to be proving to be a tough thing. The community is used to keeping secrets from humans, but not so much among themselves. It'll come out eventually, when others start to notice that human spouses aren't aging the way they should be, but I can understand why CSG want to ease people into this knowledge.

"You and Erika should come for dinner one night," I suggest. I'm not officially living with Rob yet, but only in name. I spend most weeknights at his place—it's more convenient for work, anyway—and then we both go to Here Be Dragons on the weekend so I can see my family and fly a bit and Kethe can stock us up with food.

Rob loves flying, by the way. He was hesitant at first, but after the first time we went up, he was a convert. Last week I caught him looking for properties with big yards so I'd be able to launch and land at our own home.

None of the yards were quite big enough, and we're not prepared to look at farms, even small ones, so for now it's going to be weekends only.

"We'd love that," Julian says, smiling. "I'll have a chat with her, and we'll call to sort out the details."

I start gathering my things together. Rob's taken the afternoon off work for a session with Noah, and he's going to meet me at CSG. I want to visit with people at the office anyway and talk to Grandfather "officially" about outreach services. He and King Raðulfr have committed to funding some programs, but we're still working out what they'll be, where, and how much they'll cost.

"Dustin." I turn my attention back to Julian. "I just want to make sure you know how glad Erika and I are that Rob found you. We think you're perfect for him, and we're so happy he has someone who truly understands and loves who he is."

I swallow hard and blink so tears don't even have the chance to form. That's one thing about my biped form that I'm not a fan of.

"Thank you. I know how close he and Erika are, and he thinks of you as his father, so that means a lot."

We smile at each other, and then he says, "Well, I'd better get back to work. Are you staying in town tonight or going back home?"

I shrug. "We're not sure yet. Maybe staying. There are some people I want to catch up with."

We stroll out of the boardroom and part ways with warm goodbyes. I hadn't taken the time to consider before now how lucky it is that Rob's parents are so cool. It would suck if they hated me or disapproved of our relationship. I mean, that wouldn't stop us from being together, but it's much better this way, with doting parents. I do like being doted upon.

It takes me only fifteen minutes to get from Julian's offices to the building that holds the DEA—Dragon Elf Alliance—and CSG offices. I tamp down my eagerness to see Rob—we've been apart for six whole hours—and stop first at the DEA.

"Dustin, good," Dáithí, the overlord of reception, declares when he sees me. "Your grandfather and the king want to see you. Let me just check… okay, they're both free in forty minutes, so I'll book a meeting, and until then, I have some paperwork for you, and the finance department wants to talk to you about tax loopholes."

I look around. "Do I actually work here and just not know it?"

"Ha. Ha. Do the paperwork first. I'll tell finance you'll be there in a bit." He hands me a tablet with documents already visible on screen, then reaches for his switchboard and hits a button, dismissing me.

There will be time to ponder this later. For now, I dare not get on Dáithí's bad side. He looks cute and harmless, but he has the power to make lives miserable. Never piss off a receptionist.

Of course, being the boundary-pusher I am, I test his limits just a tiny bit by leaning against his desk instead of going to find a chair.

The documents appear to be service agreements for non-employee consultants. I blink, then read through them more carefully. My name is on them and every-thing, and it looks like Grandfather and the king want me to consult on outreach support and the redesign of the current government program.

My hand might be shaking fractionally when I put the tablet down and ask Dáithí, "Don't people usually offer someone a job before having the contract drawn up?"

He doesn't look up from his screen. "Who cares? If you don't want it, don't sign it. But stop lounging all over my desk. It looks unprofessional."

I narrow my eyes and send a quick, light wash of power over his forearm. It's harmless but will feel like an annoying itch for the next few minutes. Petty, perhaps, but it makes me feel better. Then I take the tablet and sit in one of the visitor armchairs to reread the docs and think about what this means.

My next stop is down the hall in the finance depart-ment, where I'm leapt on by three people. Two of them are babbling about budgets for the new program, while the third wants to know what my fee is and whether I'm willing to negotiate it.

We set up a tentative meeting for next week—tentative because there are some things I need to sort out first—and then I escape and go find Grandfather and King Raðulfr.

They're waiting for me in the king's office.

"How did the board meeting go?" Grandfather asks before even saying hello.

"Well, thanks. Everything's on track." I raise the tablet. "What's this about?"

The king winces. "I told him we should have set up a formal meeting and discussed it with you first."

I nod. "Or at least sent me an email with a heads-up." The three of us had already talked about the gaps in the current program and what I thought was needed for the future, but that's as far as it went. I'd come away from that meeting with plans to establish my own third-party support organization funded by donors and the occasional government grant. I definitely didn't expect them to want my help overhauling the existing system.

"Apologies," Grandfather says breezily. "I was so excited, I just forged ahead. Have you read the contract?"

"Yes. It doesn't specify what you'd want to see from the new program. In other words, you're not telling me exactly what you're hiring me for."

The king smiles. "This is such a proud moment. I've despaired for so long of you ever growing up. And look at you now!" He plants his forearms on his desk and leans forward. "Let's hash it out."

And we do.

By the time we're finished, I feel a lot better. They

may be handing me this contract, but they're clearly going to make me work for it. And even if there's an element of "let's look after Dustin" here, that's okay. I can prove I don't need it.

"Dustin? One more thing," the king says as I stand.

I sit again. "Of course."

He glances at Grandfather and then takes a deep breath. "I have a confession to make."

Blinking, I mull that over. A confession? To me? "Okay?"

"Last week, I went out to Beresford University and sneaked into one of your man's lectures."

What? "Are you… thinking of getting an education in classical literature?" I don't understand.

Grandfather snorts. "He did it at my request, Dustin. You're planning to be with Rob forever, and I wanted to know if that was feasible."

It hits like a freight train, and I gasp. How could I have forgotten? The king is one of those elves with the ability to see paired souls.

My gaze flies to him as hope surges. Surely they wouldn't have raised the subject if the news was bad?

King Raðulfr smiles at me, the same affectionate, fond smile he's given me for millennia. "Your soul and Rob's are perfectly paired," he confirms, and joy explodes through my entire being.

I get into the elevator, trying to look confident and assured, *not* the slightly dazed I really am. Could this be happening? Rob and I are practically fated to be together for all eternity. And I expected it to take years before I'd be at this stage of my master career plan. The fact that it's all coming together so soon—with the added bonus of Rob—makes me wonder how I can possibly be so lucky.

The elevator door opens three floors up at the CSG offices, and I step out.

"Dustin!" Someone bursts from the stairwell beside the elevator and grabs my arm, panting. "There you are."

I blink at Hagen, who appears to have run up the stairs.

"Hi. Did you need something?"

He gasps a few times, so I wait for him to catch his breath. I like Hagen. He's one of the few dragons who works for the royal court, overseeing security in a similar position to my friend Caolan. But unlike Caolan, he can be rough around the edges. A bit smoother now that he's in love and settled into domestic bliss, but you still wouldn't call him diplomatic.

"Sorry," he manages at last, straightening. "Three flights at a dead run was not a good idea. I should probably start going to the gym more."

I squint at him. "Don't you go every day? I thought it was part of your routine."

He grins and flexes, reminding me why people call him a douchebag. "Yeah, that's right. But I don't train by running up stairs, and clearly that's an oversight."

"I'm happy to have helped identify this weakness in your training program. But… did you need something?" I really want to go find Rob. After the emotional highs of the day, I need cuddles.

He grins toothily, and I have the sudden urge to flee. "There's a rumor going around that you're roasting meat with a human."

I can't help laughing. "You're such a shit, Hagen.

Why do you keep using that expression when you know how badly it translates?"

He shrugs. "Shock value, mostly. Now tell me all about your human."

"Seriously? You ran up three flights of stairs to ask me about Rob?"

"Rob? Rob what?"

"Hagen." I put my hands on my hips and level him with a withering stare.

"Dustin," he counters, crossing his arms and quirking an eyebrow.

"Um, excuse me?"

We both turn to look at the owner of the new voice, a middle-aged succubus with her arms full of binders.

"Could I get to the elevator, please?"

"Sorry," we mumble, moving out of the way. Across the room, Candice, the demon receptionist, is giving us an exasperated look. I wave tentatively.

"All I'm saying," Hagen insists, "is that you can't keep your man to yourself."

"I fucking can," I snap, affronted at the very idea of sharing Rob. My Rob!

Hagen rolls his eyes. "Chill, okay? I'm not interested in stealing your human from you. But like it or not, you're a public figure, and the public wants to see their Prince Charming all loved up and happy. Let's start with the people here at DEA. Drinks one night."

I hesitate. "I'm not a public figure," I mumble sulkily. This is that whole stupid Prince Dustin thing again. "Grandfather's the public figure."

"Which makes you one by association. And even if you weren't, there are some of us here who like you and want to meet your boyfriend."

Awww. That's so sweet.

"And tell him about all the things you've done that he probably doesn't know."

So much for sweet.

"Rob and I don't have secrets from each other," I announce loftily, because isn't that what people say? It's a lie, of course. I've told Rob that I used to be spoiled and impetuous and wild, but I don't think he really understands what that entailed, and I definitely didn't give him any details. He loves me, and there's no need to tempt fate on that.

Hagen's so busy laughing, he can't fend me off when I pinch him.

"No secrets," he gasps, wiping tears from his eyes. "Please. As if."

"Are you saying you have secrets in your relationship?" He's been with his boyfriend, the realtor who helped us find Here Be Dragons, for over four years. The two of them practically finish each other's sentences. No way does Hagen keep anything secret.

"Not big ones," he concedes. "But stupid shit I did in the past that has no impact on my current life? Sure. He also doesn't need to know what I'm buying him for his birthday or that I've been eating chocolate here at the office even though we're both cutting back on sugar."

I purse my lips in thought. "I think he'd disagree on that last one."

Hagen nods sagely. "Probably. Which is why he never has to know. Now," he leans in, "when can we meet your boyfriend?"

There's no way I'm going to get out of this. I knew it had to happen eventually, but I'd hoped to hold it off for a while longer. I know Rob loves me, but I wanted him to be well and truly ensnared before meeting people who might scare him off.

Sighing, I say, "Let me talk to him. We'll have a barbeque or something at Here Be Dragons, but I'm not sure when yet." We can invite his parents and stepsiblings too. I haven't met Julian's kids yet, and I'd like to.

"I'll spread the word," Hagen promises, then disappears back into the stairwell before I can protest. Oh well. I do want Rob to meet more of my friends, and I'm sure they'll be on their best behavior.

Maybe.

Abandoning my increasingly panicked thoughts, I wave again to Candice, who's on the phone, and head down the hallway toward the meeting room where Rob and Noah have their training sessions. I hesitate and listen outside the door, trying to tell if things are going well or not, but I can't hear anything. Rob mentioned that Noah always wards the room so people don't barge in on them, so I knock.

A moment later, a scowling Noah opens the door. "Oh, it's you," he says, the scowl lessening slightly. "Come in."

"Who did you think it was?" I walk past him and smile at Rob, who's sitting at the table looking focused and studious. He's so sexy when he's all serious like this. It's even sexier the way he breaks into a smile when he sees me.

"My idiot boyfriend," Noah grumbles, closing the door and locking it. There's a shift in pressure, which I've learned is what it feels like when humans perform magic, and I guess he's re-warding the room.

Rob gets up from the table and comes over to kiss

me, and as I often do, I capture the kiss for my hoard. "How did the meeting go?" he murmurs, nuzzling my neck.

"Mmm."

He chuckles. "Dustin?"

I push aside the warm, fuzzy feelings of having Rob's arms around me and his lips on my skin. "Uh… yes. It went well. Really well." Stepping back, I force my brain back into gear. "How's the training going?"

Rob's face lights up. "Not too bad."

Noah snorts as he walks past us and takes a seat. "He's being modest. He might have struggled with all the meditation at the beginning, but now that he's in the groove, he's killing it."

"Really?" Hope blooms in me. The sooner he masters this, the sooner I can be sure we'll have so much more time together.

"Show him," Noah suggests to Rob.

My beloved studies me, then a moment later, a glowing ball of light appears in the air between us. I clap my hands, preparing to launch myself at him, but then it slowly changes color to a warm, rosy pink, and reshapes itself into a heart.

I put a hand over my mouth as the heart floats toward me, reshapes itself again into a pair of lips, and brushes against my cheek.

"Another kiss for your hoard," Rob murmurs, and tears well up in my eyes. "What? No! Don't be upset," he exclaims, and the lips vanish.

I dash away the tears with a choked sob/laugh as he closes the distance between us and puts his arms around me. "I'm not upset," I promise, snuggling against him.

"I'm so happy. And you're so romantic. How did I get this lucky?"

"Uh, guys, you know I'm still here, right?" Noah interrupts, and we both turn to look at him.

"Oh yeah," I say. "Sure. I knew you were here. Of course." Just as well I didn't go with my first instinct to strip Rob naked and cover him with kisses. I take a precautionary step away from Rob so I'm not tempted.

Noah rolls his eyes. "Yeah, whatever."

CHAPTER SEVENTEEN

Rob

MY TUTOR, who's the same age as some of my grad students, rolls his eyes in a way that makes me feel a million years old.

"Yeah, whatever," he says. "Anyway, as you saw, Rob's got this magic thing whipped."

"Sometimes," I add, because even though I'm doing a lot better now, there are still some things that escape me. But given how much I struggled with the initial meditation, what I can do now feels like conquering Everest. Those first few weeks, I was convinced I'd never get the hang of it. No matter how much I tried, I just couldn't feel the existential magic that Noah kept insisting was right there. I was careful not to let Dustin see how discouraged I was, but at one point I resigned myself to the fact that I'd only have another forty years with him after all.

Then it all fell into place.

Maybe I was just trying too hard. I'll never know, but once I felt the pulse of the magic for the first time, the ebb and flow of it around me, that was it. I can feel it all the time now, a background presence ready for me to draw on when I need it. The actual drawing-on part isn't always easy, but my "magic muscles," as Noah calls them, are getting stronger, and the more I practice, the more I'm able to do. It's *amazing*. A total dream come true.

Noah started out as a really strict teacher, but he relaxed a lot once he saw how determined I am and how much I've been practicing outside our lessons. We had a very long and detailed discussion about how human magic use actually works, that it's essentially wish fulfilment and that we need to "be careful what we wish for," followed by the horror story of how he almost died when he tried to do something the human body isn't designed for. Since the main reason I'm doing this is to prolong my life, I'll be abso-fucking-lutely careful about everything I use magic for.

"You're doing great," Dustin says, smiling adoringly at me. I really love when he gets that look. It makes me feel like a god.

"You really are," Noah adds before I can protest again. "Stop with the whole insecure thing. I'd tell you if you sucked."

"He would," Dustin agrees, going over to the table and sitting down. "Noah's upfront like that."

Okay then.

"In another few weeks, you should be able to learn how to redirect magic so it's constantly healing you. That's what will keep you from aging," Noah explains. "It's a pretty simple process, but I want to make sure you've got a good gauge on what healthy magic use feels like and what the warning signs of overuse are."

"I'm good with that." I want to do this right. "I'm

having fun in the meantime," I add. It's true. Aside from cute tricks like what I just showed Dustin, I'm learning all sorts of little things that will be immeasurably helpful in day-to-day life, plus some bigger things that challenge my brain. I'd forgotten how much fun learning something new can be.

Noah and Dustin start talking about the differences in their approaches to magic use, and I listen with only half my attention. It's fascinating that there can be so many different ways to use magic—although I suppose only the human method truly "uses" magic in the sense of directing the existential force that makes up the universe. Sorcerers draw from their own inner power that they're born with and then "weave" it to do what they want. I've never truly understood how that works. Elf spellcasting is closer to what humans do. The way it's been explained to me is that it's a combination of sorcerer weaving and human manipulation. They draw on both their inner power and existential magic and mix the two. And dragons... well, they're completely different from anything else. I've learned a lot about dragons since hooking up with Dustin. For one thing, unlike our Earth shifter species, dragons aren't technically shifters. They *choose* to shift into biped forms so they can hang out with other species. Over the millennia, they've gotten used to the things they can do as bipeds that they can't do in dragon form—like sex, and wow, I had so many questions after that revelation—so now it's just a natural part of their lives, but they're not naturally half-half the way our Earth shifters are.

In fact, they're not naturally corporeal beings at all. When I showed interest in dragon history, Fabian treated me to a quick overview of their origins. The first hundred or so generations of dragons were entirely ethereal, made up purely of energy—the way Fabian described it, electrical impulses of some kind, although that's not really my area of expertise. They were messing around one day and realized they could convert their self-energy into solid matter, and over several generations decided it was more fun to be corporeal than not. Even though they're no longer able to become ethereal, they're still beings of energy and can do things that no other species can because of that. It's awe-inspiring and also kind of frightening to know what kind of power can be wielded by beings who squabble over which vegetable would make a better superhero if vegetables could be superheroes. Spoiler alert: nobody picked broccoli.

This is my life now, and I'm loving it. I'm not going to lie, I was worried at first. Even though I knew Dustin genuinely didn't need a college education and had other things he wanted to spend his time on, it was instinctive for me to feel guilty about it. But seeing how happy he's been this past month since he dropped out has gone a long way toward making me feel better. He's so enthusiastic about and dedicated to his youth outreach programs. Making him stay in college and being apart for another two years makes no sense under these circumstances.

Of course, my logic doesn't make quite as much sense to others. When Gerald found out Dustin had dropped his class and dropped out of college entirely, he came to see me, *very* concerned. Since I have no intention of hiding Dustin's presence in my life, I had to explain that yes, Dustin and I are now together. Gerald was not impressed. Even though I told him that Dustin was planning to join the "family business" and that his college degree had just been for the fun of the college experience, the whole age-gap, teacher-student thing was too much for him. And of course I couldn't tell him that Dustin is in fact a four-thousand-year-old dragon with plenty of life experience. So our friendship is now very strained.

I'm sorry about that, but I can't regret having Dustin in my life. It's only been a short time, and there's a dubious little voice at the back of my mind muttering things about honeymoon periods, but I've been in relationships before, and they've never been like this. Even when they were in that wonderful first flush, I didn't have the sense of bone-deep comfort that I do with Dustin.

I smile fondly at him, and, as if sensing my attention, he glances over. His whole face changes when he sees me looking, his eyes lighting up, lips pouting, a light flush of color creeping into his cheeks.

"You two are pathetic," Noah observes. "Go home and get it out of your systems."

I laugh in embarrassment, heat flushing through me. "Whoops. Sorry, Noah." I feel like a teenager again, caught making out with my boyfriend by my parents.

"Don't apologize to him," Dustin says. "What we feel is beautiful."

I can't deny that.

MUCH LATER THAT NIGHT, I lie back against my pillow and focus on the three lightballs floating above me. This is a super simple exercise, akin to stretching, but I need it to be second nature—the kind of thing that comes as naturally as breathing. I need to maintain those lightballs without conscious thought… like, while I'm sleeping. When I can constantly run a low-grade spell like that in the background, I'll be ready to start work on the healing spell that will prolong my life.

I haven't managed it yet—the lightballs are always gone when I wake in the morning—but I'm determined.

Footsteps pad down the hallway, and I look over at the door as Dustin appears.

"Sorry that took so long," he says, stripping and dropping his clothes on the floor before climbing into bed.

I sigh.

He sighs.

Then he gets out of bed, scoops up his abandoned clothes, and dumps them on the chair in the corner.

"Better?" he asks, hands planted defiantly on his hips. I let my gaze skim over his beautiful, lithe body, pausing when I reach his already semihard cock.

"Thank you."

He sniffs and gets back into bed. "Only for you would I get up to move clothes. You're lucky I love you."

I've heard him say those words so many times, but they never fail to warm me from the inside out. I know now that he means them. I know that the energy that makes him up recognized something in me when he first saw me, and that even before he knew me, he loved me. It's the most amazing feeling. And he shows me his love in a million tiny ways—like getting out of bed to put his clothes on the chair when he could have easily done it with magic. Honestly, I wouldn't care if he did use magic to do it. I just don't want to trip over his pants if I get up to go to the bathroom in the middle of the night. But for him, expending that little bit of extra effort is a declaration of his feelings for me, and I can't help but adore him for it.

"How'd you go?" I ask, wanting to get it out of the way before we get distracted. It's already hard enough to think when he's naked beside me.

He grumbles. "It's going to take some work. Mostly paperwork. Maybe some bribes."

I wince. Bribes have long played a part in keeping the community a secret from humans and still allowing them to receive the support they need, and fuck knows human bureaucracy is built on bribes, but there's a part of me that still hates it. I guess all that time spent with classic literature and pure-hearted characters has had a bigger impact on me than I thought.

Dustin's spent most of the evening on the phone with town councilors, trying to cut through the last of the red tape to get the site approved for his first outreach center. It's good to go in principle, but they seem to be dragging their feet on the final sign-off. It probably doesn't help that Dustin's had to fudge some of the information—giving humans all the details of a youth center for nonhumans would probably be a bad idea.

But my guy is proving worthy of the task he's taken on.

"Are you still going to be opening in December? I know you're looking forward to singing holiday songs with grumpy teenagers." Though for the life of me, I can't imagine why.

"Still on track," he confirms. "But even if we get delayed, I can get my fill at your mom's caroling party."

My gut freezes. "What caroling party?" Mom quit

hosting those almost twenty years ago. She said the hell-hounds were too competitive. Because yes, hellhounds manage to make carol singing into a competition.

I can't imagine dragons will be any better.

"Oh, she was telling me about the caroling parties she used to throw, and it sounded like so much fun that I convinced her to add one to the itinerary this year." He gets onto his knees and bounces excitedly, which normally I would be very interested in, but... caroling party.

"Greaaat," I murmur.

He laughs. "How about this? For every carol we sing at the party, I'll give you a blowjob, time and place of your choosing."

Annnnnnd I'm hard. I clear my throat. "You'd do that anyway," I point out, because Dustin's very generous when it comes to my cock.

"True," he agrees. "Hmm, what can I bribe you with, then? Toys? Costumes? Handcuffs?"

I purse my lips to hide my smile. "We've done all that."

He gasps dramatically and puts the back of his hand to his forehead. "We have? Oh no, is our sex life getting stale?"

My laugh is impossible to hold back, and I lunge forward to grab him and drag him into my lap. "I love you. I don't need bribes to do things that make you happy," I murmur between kisses. He's hoarding them, and the brightly colored evidence of my love for him is fluttering around our heads. He'll never be able to doubt how much I want him.

Not for all eternity.

Thanks for reading *The Professor's Dragon*! Want the bonus scene where Dustin discovers the Christmas season? Subscribe to my monthly newsletter: bit.ly/ LouisaMBonus and download it now!

We talk spoilers in my Facebook Reader Group, RoMMance With Becca & Louisa.

If you're curious about Fabian's purity ring, don't worry, you get the whole story in *The Dragon Experiment*.

For early access to chapters of my upcoming books, artwork, and other bonus material, check out my Patreon here: patreon.com/louisamasters

ALSO BY LOUISA MASTERS

Saddles & Suits
Alistair's Extraordinaries
Grave Situation
Elemental Men: The Complete Series

Style Me
Rebrand
Couture

Elf Magic
Wooing the Wiccan
Enticing the Elf

The Collective
Higher Demon
Demon Hunter

Demons-In-Law
Asher
Micah
Zachary

Franklin U
Mr. Romance
The Holigay Hookup *related novella
Batting Style

Ghostly Guardians

Spirited Situation

Vortex Conundrum

Conduit Crisis

Gateway Catastrophe

Here Be Dragons

Dragon Ever After

The Professor's Dragon

The Dragon Experiment

Conspiracy of Dragons

Hidden Species

Demons Do It Better

One Bite With A Vampire

Hijinks With A Hellhound

Sorcerers Always Satisfy

Hidden Species Box Set

Met His Match

Charming Him

Offside Rules

A Christmas Chance (novella)

Between the Covers (M/F)

Joy Universe

I've Got This

Follow My Lead

In Your Hands

<u>Take Us There</u>

Novellas

Fake It 'Til You Make It (permafree)

One Golden Night

O Hell, All Ye Shoppers

Out of the Office

After the Blaze

Blokes Down Under Novella Collection

Louisa Masters started reading romance much earlier than her mother thought she should. As an adult, she feeds her addiction in every spare second. She spent years trying to build a "sensible" career, working in bookstores, recruitment, resource management, administration, and as a travel agent before finally conceding defeat and devoting herself to the world of romance novels.

Louisa has a long list of places first discovered in books that she wants to visit, and every so often she overcomes her loathing of jet lag and takes a trip that charges her imagination. She lives in Melbourne, Australia, where she whines about the weather for most of the year while secretly admitting she'll probably never move.

http://www.louisamasters.com

www.ingramcontent.com/pod-product-compliance
Lightning Source LLC
Chambersburg PA
CBHW032000050726

47590CB00006B/1985